I0596773

BOOTS & ROSES

UGLY STICK SALOON SERIES #8

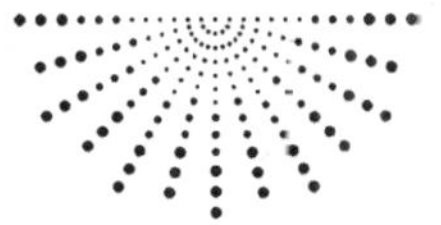

MYLA JACKSON

TWISTED PAGE INC

BOOTS & ROSES

UGLY STICK SALOON SERIES #8

New York Times & USA Today
Bestselling Author

ELLE JAMES

writing as

MYLA JACKSON

Copyright © 2017 by Myla Jackson

Copyright © 2014 by Myla Jackson

Originally published by Samhain in Dec 2014

All rights reserved.

No part of this book may be reproduced in any form or by any electronic or mechanical means, including information storage and retrieval systems, without written permission from the author, except for the use of brief quotations in a book review.

EBOOK ISBN: 978-1-62695-093-1

PRINT ISBN: 978-1-62695-095-5

Dedicated to all my readers who keep the Ugly Stick Saloon alive! Thank you for reading!

Enjoy other Ugly Stick Saloon books by Myla Jackson
Ugly Stick Saloon Series
Boots & Chaps (#1)
Boots & Sex Ed (#2)
Boots & Leather (#3)
Boots & Promises (#4)
Boots & Bareback (#5)
Boots & Dirty Tricks (#6)
Boots & Lace (#7)
Boots & Roses (#8)
Boots & Buckles (#9)
Boots & the Wishes (#10)
Boots & Twisters (#11)
Boots & the Bachelor (#12)
Boots & The Rogue (#13)
Boots & The Heartbreaker (#14)
Boots & Wings (#15)

Visit Mylajackson.com for more information
Visit her alter ego Elle James at ellejames.com
Join Elle James and Myla Jackson's Newsletter at
http://ellejames.com/ElleContact.htm

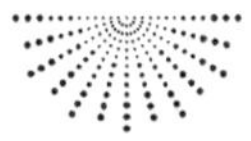

"The Women's Aid Society should make a killing off this fundraiser." Bunny Leigh sat with her back to the bar, her gaze glued to the stage. Despite her best effort to remain detached, she couldn't help but get caught up in the insanity going on around her at the Annual Cowboy Auction.

"No kidding." Charli Sutton paused long enough at the bar to drop the dirty glasses and order the next round for the tables she waited. "You did a great job on the decorations."

Bunny shrugged. "It's the least the Sweet Temptations Flower Shop could do. Heck, Audrey offered up the Ugly Stick Saloon for the event, and giving away one free drink per customer was brilliant."

"Yeah, the drinks will grease the wheels for bidding. Her crowning glories were recruiting the cowboys..." Charli nodded toward the exit, "...and hiring the hottest deputy in the tri-county area to keep it sane."

Bunny glanced at Jack Monahan, the best-looking deputy on the sheriff's force, and her cheeks heated. He'd stopped by her flower shop on a regular basis to buy flowers for his mother. What a guy. Sensitive and handsome, with his dark hair and big brown eyes rimmed with lashes a girl would give her eyeteeth for. If Bunny was interested in dating, he'd be one of the local bachelors at the top of her list. Not that he'd be interested, and Bunny wasn't the type of girl to ask and risk rejection.

Two years since her divorce seemed too soon for Bunny to get used to the idea of dating again. Yet two years had been plenty of time for her ex to take the plunge. The bastard was getting married, already. Not that she cared about Ray anymore. Not since he'd cheated on her with the cute little dental hygienist he was now engaged to.

With a sigh, Bunny dragged her gaze from Jack and stared down at the program, running through the list of names. "Wow, she really struck gold. I don't think I've ever seen such a great lineup."

"Yeah." Charli smiled. "It's too bad I'm engaged, or I'd bid."

Bunny's brows rose, a smile curling her lips. "What, you don't think Connor would let you go out on a little ol' date with one of them?"

"Not no, but hell no." Charli frowned. "I may be taken, but there are a lot of single women in this room who aren't. And I know for a fact some of them have been savin' all year for this."

Bunny panned the room. Women of all shapes and sizes crowded every bit of floor space in the saloon, each carrying a paddle with a number on it, ready for when the bidding started.

"Gotta get back to work. Everyone's already gone through their first-round freebie. They're into round two, and the fun hasn't even started." Charli grabbed a tray of beer mugs and hurried back out into the sea of raging estrogen.

Audrey Anderson, the owner of the Ugly Stick, leaned over the bar. "Can I get you another beer?"

Bunny stared at her mug, surprised to see it was empty. "Sure. But it'll have to be my last. I have to drive."

"No worries. The Gray Wolf brothers are lined up to provide free rides home to anyone who isn't fit to drive."

"Thanks." Bunny smiled. "We'll see how it goes." She'd never had so much to drink that she couldn't drive. She didn't plan on it now.

Audrey filled Bunny's mug from the tap and set it on the bar in front of her. "Where's your number?"

Bunny snorted. "Don't need one. I'm not bidding."

"What?" Audrey shook her head. "You've been divorced for two years now. It's about time you started dating again."

With another sigh, Bunny lifted her mug and sipped the golden brew before responding. "After the disaster of my marriage, why would I want to jump back into a relationship? I like where I am in life. I don't need a man to make me happy."

"Ray Zinke was a jerk. You did the right thing by divorcing him," Audrey said, as she wiped the bar with a clean rag. "Besides, not every man is a dirt bag like Ray. Look at Jackson. He's one hundred percent awesome. And his brothers Luke and Mark rank right up there with him."

Although Bunny had thought about the Gray Wolf twins and their swarthy, Native American good looks, she'd learned by experience that looks weren't everything. And unfortunately, Libby the bartender had the corner on the twin market. "They're taken."

"Maybe so, but they're good examples that not all men are cut of the same dumbass cloth. You have to give other men a chance."

Bunny shook her head. "No, I don't."

"What about companionship?"

"I can get a dog," Bunny was quick to quip, but there was the rub. A dog might be good company, but she missed having someone to talk to at night after work. Someone to hold her and whisper sweet nothings in her ear.

Audrey frowned. "What about partnership? Someone to share your life?"

"I almost lost half my business to Ray when he left me. I'm still paying him back a little at time and probably will be paying for the next decade. No partners."

With a soft harrumph Audrey shot back, "Okay… what about sex?"

"I own a nifty array of vibrators." Bunny lifted her

chin, daring Audrey to challenge her lie. She only had one. "I can have sex any time I want. I'm responsible for my own orgasms, thank you very much."

Audrey frowned. "It's not the same."

"Audrey, I'm not looking for a man in my life right now." Bunny might not have been looking, but Audrey was hitting too close to home. The last couple of weeks, she'd been in the dumps going home to an empty apartment every night. No one to talk to. No one to share her day with.

"Well, if you change your mind, I took the liberty of signing you up for the auction." Audrey slapped a numbered paddle on the counter. "Think about it. It's just a date." She walked away, shaking her head.

Bunny sighed. Why couldn't people believe she was happy living alone?

Because you're not.

The thought came out of the blue and wedged in Bunny's craw, bringing her down when she should have been enjoying the anticipation of the auction's kickoff. She loved watching the bachelor cowboys roped into participating. The area had its fair share of handsome, single men, although they seemed to be getting younger every year.

Another sigh escaped Bunny's lips.

"Hey, pretty lady, what's gotcha down?" a warm, sexy voice said behind her.

She turned toward the bar and smiled at Cory McBride, her part-time flower deliveryman. "Just thinking."

"If you're thinking about me, I'd hope the frown

would turn upside down." He winked and smiled, his full, sensuous lips curling ever so slightly.

Enough to make Bunny want to taste them.

Holy hell! I didn't just think that, did I?

"No, I was just trying to decide whether I would bid on a cowboy."

"Then save your money for me." He puffed out his chest, which was clad in a crisp white shirt that disappeared into neatly ironed blue jeans. The ridge beneath his fly stood out against the soft, dark denim. "I'm one of the cowboys being auctioned, along with a special surprise."

Bunny's heart flipped against her ribs and her belly tightened. She'd had a secret lust for this young man since he'd started working for her several months ago.

Her gaze slid over his broad shoulders and down to his narrow waist. Not that he was a boy. At twenty-one, he was more of a man than her ex-husband had ever been, and Cory was proud of his body, not at all shy about showing off the rippling muscles and taut abs.

And he had a lot of reasons to be proud of that glorious body.

Bunny dropped her gaze to her beer, afraid Cory would see his boss drooling if she didn't get a grip on her unfulfilled longing. "I'll leave the bidding to the younger girls. Can't have Temptation calling me a cougar now, can I?" She smiled up at him and immediately regretted it.

Cory's eyes narrowed. "What, you're all of twenty-six?"

"Not that it's any of your business." She ran her finger along the rim of her mug. "I'm twenty-seven." She held her breath, waiting for his gasp. It didn't come.

He shook his head. "You're not old."

"Older than you." She sighed. Damn she'd done a lot of that this evening. What was wrong with her? "I've been married and divorced, and I own my own business. I feel like Methuselah."

"Hardly. For the record, there's only a little more than five years difference in our ages. And although I haven't been married and divorced, I've owned my own business since I was nineteen."

Bunny frowned. "Really?"

Cory's lips spread in a sensuous smile. "I'm a waiter and stripper here at the Ugly Stick, but I've been investing my money since I started working and have quite a personal portfolio. I'm financially independent. And, as you know, I just graduated with my degree in pre-med biology and I'm heading to medical school in Dallas next fall."

"Yeah, I know. I'll be losing my deliveryman." She sighed. Having Cory around had been fun, and the shop wouldn't be the same without his smiling face. "That's quite the resume. But that doesn't erase the fact I'm five years older than you."

"Look, sweetheart, between you and me..." He leaned across the bar, his face inches from hers. Cory's thick, golden mane flowed down around his shoulders, and blue eyes as clear as a summer day shined into hers. "I'd rather go out with you than any other woman in this place."

Suddenly unable to breathe, Bunny closed her gaping mouth and licked her lips. The scent of his aftershave swirled around her and made her want to tip forward and plant her lips on his.

He winked. "Don't sell yourself short, darlin'. You've got a lot more to offer than a twenty-one-year-old." Cory leaned closer and kissed her startled lips, then straightened. "You are a beautiful, warm and generous woman. What's not to love?"

Her mouth tingled from where his lips had touched, and she clenched her fingers to keep from reaching across the counter and claiming a do-over on that brief kiss.

"Now, if you'll pardon me, I have to go get undressed for my turn on the stage." He tapped her numbered paddle. "Think about it."

How the hell could she think with her brain fried by one little brush of his lips?

Charli swung by, her eyes wide. "Did I see what I think I saw?"

Heat climbed up Bunny's neck and into her cheeks. "No. No, you didn't see anything."

"I did! Cory kissed you, didn't he?" Charli dropped her tray on the counter and gave her order to Libby, before turning to grab Bunny's hands. "He never comes on to women. They always come on to him."

"So?" Bunny pushed her hair behind her ear. "He

delivers flowers for me. It was just a friendly peck, like a handshake."

"My rosy butt it was." Charli's face split into a wide grin. "What did he say to go with that kiss?"

"Nothing," Bunny lied. "It wasn't a kiss." She lifted her mug to her lips, hoping it would give Charli the hint that she didn't want to discuss Cory anymore.

"You have to bid on him," Charli insisted, hiking her tray of drinks onto her shoulder.

"I don't have to do any such thing."

The band struck up a tune.

Charli's head jerked up and she set her full tray back on the counter. "Ah, that's my cue. I'm the MC."

Bunny sucked in a deep breath and let it out. *Whew. Saved by the music.*

Audrey hurried forward. "I'll get your orders, Charli. Get on out there before the women riot."

"Goin'." Charli nodded toward Bunny as she passed. "Make sure she bids on Cory. He kissed her."

Audrey's brows rose. "Cory kissed you?"

Bunny wanted to trip Charli for her parting comment. Now she'd have to face the Audrey inquisition. She raised her hand. "Please. It was just a peck. We're only friends."

With a laugh, Audrey gathered the tray Libby had filled with beer mugs and glasses of wine. "Okay. I get it. Don't push you. Still, if not Cory, consider bidding on someone else. There are plenty of handsome cowboys who will be strutting their boots and buckles across the stage." Audrey took off, carrying the heavy tray as if it weighed nothing, her long strawberry blond hair swaying sassily.

Alone in a saloon full of women, Bunny watched as one cowboy after another stood on the stage, removed his shirt and played up the crowd. The shouts and screams grew louder as the liquor flowed and bidding became more intense.

Twice, Deputy Jack Monahan had to break up a fight between several of the women. He was starting to look a little harried since he'd had his ass pinched on more than one occasion.

Bunny found herself wishing she was close enough to pinch as well. As soon as the thought crossed her mind, she straightened. She'd drooled over two handsome men tonight. Like Audrey said, she probably needed to get out more often. Maybe it was time for her to start dating again. Hell, Ray was getting married in three days. He'd definitely moved on. Why not her?

After the first couple of men were auctioned, Jack made his way to the bar where Bunny sat.

"Can a guy get an ice cold…water?" He sighed. "Rather have a beer, but I'm afraid the ladies would take advantage of me."

Libby chuckled, handing Jack a mug of ice water. "Audrey needs to hire ugly cops for this party. You're too damned good looking to keep the peace."

The man is riot material, Bunny added silently. Her body flushed with heat at the deputy's nearness, and she struggled for something to say.

Jack leaned across Bunny and snagged the mug in

his fist, his broad shoulders filling her vision. "Mind if I sit?" He eased onto the stool beside Bunny. "Gonna bid tonight?"

Sitting beside the handsome deputy, Bunny's heartbeat fluttered for the second time that night. "I hadn't planned on it."

Jack winked. "Be a shame. I know for a fact any one of those cowboys would be proud as punch to be bought and paid for by you." He set his mug down and tapped his chest. "Why, if I was gonna be up there, I'd hope and pray it was your paddle rising to stake a claim on me."

Bunny's gut knotted, and her body trembled at his softly spoken words. She reminded herself there were a lot of prettier women in the saloon. and her lips twisted. "I bet you've told half the women in this bar the same thing. Did Audrey put you up to advertising as well as busting up fights?"

He raised his hand Boy Scout style and shook his head. "No one put me up to it. You're the first woman I've said that to and the last." He leaned close until his lips almost brushed her ear. "You're the only florist I buy my roses from."

"Jack, I'm the only florist in town." Bunny crossed her arms. "You're in my shop at least once a week, supposedly buying flowers for your mother. How many girlfriends are you really buying for?"

A dark shadow flashed in his eyes, and his smile slipped for a second then was back in full force. "That's for me to know and you to find out." He winked, tossed back another long swallow of water and stood. "If you'll excuse me, I have a job to do." Jack lifted her hand and gazed into her eyes. "Just for the record, you're the prettiest woman in this joint."

Heat rose up Bunny's neck into her cheeks. "Liar."

His eyes narrowed. "Another one for the record…I never lie." He pressed his lips to her fingers and warmth spread throughout Bunny's body.

Out of the corner of her eyes, she could see the women on either side of her gaping, and more heat burned into her cheeks.

Jack lifted his head and brushed his lips across hers, then captured her bottom lip in between his teeth, sucking it into his warm, wet mouth. When he let go, he smiled. "That's just a sample."

Too stunned to form a coherent comeback, Bunny licked her lip in dumb silence, her gaze following Jack across the crowded floor until he was swallowed up in the surge of women.

Two men had flirted with her in one night. An anomaly for sure, but a great boost to her otherwise faltering ego. Maybe coming to the Ugly Stick Saloon had been a good idea after all. It was helping take her mind off the two-year anniversary of her divorce and her ex's pending nuptials.

CORY TIGHTENED his chaps in the dressing room behind the stage, his lips still tingling from the kiss he'd given Bunny. He'd wanted to run his hand through her long, silky brown hair and tug just enough to expose the beating pulse at the base of her throat. And that was just the beginning of all the things he wanted to do with her.

"Hey, no fair on kissin' my girl." Jack stood at the entrance to the backstage area, his arms crossed over his uniformed chest.

"Told you I was serious about making my move."

"Yeah, but did you have to kiss her?"

Cory grinned. "I wanted her to be certain of my intentions." He crammed a cowboy hat on his head and stood straight. "I only have a couple weeks before I head to Dallas for med school."

Jack shook his head. "Then why get involved now? I thought you were gonna stay single until you were through all that."

Cory's lips tightened. "For the first time in my life, I know what I want."

Jack sighed. "Bunny?"

With a nod, Cory slipped a vest over his broad chest. "If I wait until I'm through med school, she could go off and marry someone else. I have to let her know how I feel now. If she's even slightly interested, maybe she'll wait."

"What about me?" Jack spread his hands wide. "You and I both know I don't buy flowers for my mother. She's allergic."

"Look, I know you like her." Cory stared at his friend. "If you want her and she wants you, I'll step back and leave it at that. You're the best friend I've ever had, and I'd want both of you to be happy. But if I have even a smidgeon of a chance with her, I'm going for it."

"How 'bout letting her choose?"

"That's kinda what I had in mind." Cory grinned. "You and I have shared a woman before. But this is different. I want something long term. I want to know she'll be there for me, to go the distance."

"And I don't?"

Cory shrugged. "You haven't had a steady relationship since before I knew you."

Jack tipped his head. "Just because I haven't had a steady woman, doesn't mean I don't want one."

"Are you tellin' me you're over what happened to Stacy?"

Jack's lips tightened and he glanced to the far corner.

"Sorry." Cory laid a hand on his arm. "I know it hurts to talk about her."

Stacy had been Jack's girlfriend in college. They'd been inseparable from the moment they'd met. She'd died in a senseless accident that almost cost Jack his own life. When he'd woken up a week later, he'd missed the funeral. He'd also missed any opportunity for closure or goodbyes.

Jack had dropped out of school and gone to work. Stripping. He'd been on a collision course with hell until he met Cory.

Jack shook off Cory's hand and stepped away. "I don't really think I'll ever be over her. But that doesn't mean I can't get on with my life."

Cory slung an arm over Jack's shoulder. "There's not much I won't share with you, man, but Bunny is special."

"Don't I know it." Jack glanced across at Cory. "Since Stacy died, Bunny's the first woman I can't forget about when I close my eyes at night. I'm one kick in the pants short of falling in love with her, if I haven't already."

Cory nodded. "Then we have a problem."

Jack frowned. "Yeah, both of us want her, but only one of us can have her—if the woman is amenable."

Cory stared straight ahead. "You and I have been pretty close, gone through a lot together and been there for each other, right?"

With a nod, Jack answered, "Yup."

"You taught me how to defend myself."

Jack rubbed the back of his neck. "And you kicked my ass until I went back to school and finished my degree."

"We're so close we're joined at the hip in investments, and we're goin' in half on the same piece of property."

"Yeah. So?"

"What do you say we give Bunny the choice? If she's willing, she can have either one of us…or both."

His frown deepening, Jack seemed to chew on Cory's words before he responded. "I know we shared Maxy Palmer last year when we went to Fiesta in San Antonio. It was fun and all, but this is Bunny we're talkin' about, not a one-night stand."

"I know that." God, he knew that. "And I don't want to scare her off any more than you do."

"Then how's this gonna work?"

"I'm not exactly sure, but Mark and Luke Gray

Wolf share Libby and she seems more than happy with the arrangement," Cory said. "I don't see why we can't share Bunny."

Jack's lips twisted. "From what I've seen of Bunny, she's not as free-spirited or streetwise as Libby. I don't think she'll go for it."

Cory let his arm drop from Jack's shoulders and turned to face his friend, the idea blossoming. "It only makes sense. We're both interested in her, right?"

Jack nodded. "Looks that way."

"We're as close as two men can get." Cory grinned. "Hell, you're family, like my brother Nick."

"Same to you, man." Jack's lips lifted in a half-cocked smile. "So you think we can share Bunny and not jack up our friendship?"

"I can, if you can." Cory stuck out his hand. "But it's still up to Bunny."

Jack stared at Cory's hand, then gripped it in a firm handshake. "Deal." He pulled Cory into a bear hug.

Cory pulled back and clapped his hands together. "We got us a woman to court."

"How are we gonna do that?" Jack asked.

A slow smile slid across Cory's face. "It's all part of my plan."

Jack frowned. "I was afraid of that."

For forty-five minutes, Bunny left the paddle on the bar, refusing to give in to her loneliness and bid on a paid-for pity date. One by one the men paraded around the stage, women bid and the gavel banged. One by one the chance for a date passed and Bunny slipped deeper into a blue funk.

Her lips still tingled from the contact with Cory's and Jack's, and she raised her hand to touch her mouth. No vibrator had affected her as much as those earth-shaking kisses. Once again, Bunny considered Audrey's words. Maybe it was time for her to get out in the dating pool again and give love a second chance.

"Hold on to your belt buckles, ladies," Charli said with a flourish. "Here to introduce the final act, the woman who made the Cowboy Auction possible, Audrey Anderson."

Audrey stepped up on the stage with Deputy Monahan holding her arm. The owner of the Ugly Stick Saloon took the microphone from Charli and faced the crowd, her face straight, serious. "Ladies, it's been brought to my attention that we've had several instances of sexual misconduct against our own Deputy Jack Monahan. I ask you to please keep your hands to yourself and respect the man who was brought here to keep the peace."

One woman yelled, "Boo!"

The room full of women joined her, all shouting, "Boo!"

Bunny smiled. If she wasn't mistaken, Audrey had something up her sleeve and she was playing the audience.

Audrey winked. "Oh, so you like playing dirty?"

As one, the women yelled, "Hell, yeah!"

"Then let's raise the stakes. For the first time in Cowboy Auction history, we're offering up a two-fer."

The ladies roared their approval.

Despite her resolve to remain unaffected by the goings on in the saloon, Bunny leaned forward, a tingle of anticipation rippling through her body. Cory hadn't been offered up for auction yet and he'd hinted at a surprise. Was this it?

"All our cowboys have been fabulous sports about this auction, but the last bidding opportunity we're offering tonight is special and near and dear to my heart. Please welcome the two-fer deal of Cory 'The stripper so hot you'll singe your fingers' McBride..."

Cory danced out on the stage, wearing a vest, boots and leather chaps over a black G-string. The only thing not showing was his package, and it was swelled enough to give every woman enough information to go on. The man was hung.

Bunny sucked in a breath and held it while her pulse pounded so loud she could barely hear herself think. Her deliveryman had been in her sex dreams and fantasies more and more often lately. Now this... Holy smokin' cowboys!

Audrey continued, "The other half of this dynamic duo is our very own man of peace, Deputy 'Pull over and let me frisk you' Jack Monahan!" Audrey handed the microphone back to Charli.

Deputy Monahan joined Cory center stage, slipping his uniform shirt off, exposing shoulders as broad as Cory's and equally tanned and gleaming with a fine layer of oil.

Holy rock stars! Between the Adonis blond beauty that was Cory and the dark, rugged sex appeal of Jack, Bunny could barely breathe.

The crowd exploded in a frenzy, all the paddles raising in the air as the bidding started.

Bunny perched on the edge of her stool, her body trembling.

The two men danced around the stage in sync to bump-and-grind music barely audible over the cacophony of women yelling and whistling.

Bidding started at five hundred dollars and shot up from there.

Not that I'm interested in bidding. Bunny mentally calculated what she had in her bank account.

Audrey handed the numbered paddle to Bunny. "I'll match you dollar for dollar." She shrugged. "I won't keep one of them, but I want to contribute to the cause. This way I can, and Jackson won't have heartburn about it."

"I can't bid on those two. I wouldn't know what to do with one man, much less two!"

Audrey's brows rose. "Seriously? Oh, honey, you really do need to get out more often. Did I ever tell you about the day I danced for Jackson, Mark and Luke on Jackson's thirtieth birthday?" She tugged at the front of her shirt. "And I don't mean two-stepping." Audrey fanned herself. "Making me hot just thinkin' about it."

"Audrey, you're much more free-spirited. I'm... I'm..." Bunny glanced down at the paddle in her hand. "Not."

A soft hand rested on Bunny's shoulder and Audrey leaned close. "How do you know if you've never tried to be?"

Bunny shrugged. "I've always focused on getting my business going, getting my finances straight—"

"Puttin' your lousy ex-husband through school. Yeah, I can see where that gotcha." Audrey shook her head. "That's all well and good when it comes to running a business, but what about givin' yourself a second chance at love?"

"I don't need a second chance. Once was bad enough. I don't think I'm ready to float that boat again." Although the two men on the stage could more than set her sails. Holy hell, they were built like brick houses, all muscle—hard, finely chiseled muscle.

"If not for love, then date for fun or a release from stress." Audrey threw her hand in the air. "Why not satisfy your sexual fantasies? Anything to get you out of your shell, girlfriend."

"One thousand dollars!" Charli shouted into the microphone. "Ladies, this is twice the spice for the money. Don't stop now." She nodded toward the throng. "One thousand one hundred from number forty-one."

"A thousand dollars?" Bunny did the math in her head. "I'd have to sell a lot of roses to afford those two."

"Raise your paddle. Remember, I'll double whatever you can afford."

Even as Bunny shook her head, her fingers tightened around the paddle's wooden stick. "I can't."

"Yes. You can. It's just a date," Audrey insisted. "Think about what Cory can do with that whip. And Jack has handcuffs."

Cory cracked the whip, and number thirty-seven raised her paddle, bumping the bid up another one hundred dollars.

Bunny's heartbeat accelerated. She had over two grand in savings for a rainy day and maybe to pay off her ex when she got a little more saved. That money was not earmarked for a hot date with two sexy men.

It still galled her to no end that Ray got half of her business in the divorce, Texas being a community property state. Out of the "goodness of his heart" Ray had let her keep the flower shop as long as she paid him for his half over time, as a loan. He never let her forget it either, always giving her his unwanted opinion on how to run the flower shop. Spending so much money on a date would have him questioning her ability to stay in business. He might even foreclose on his loan.

"Going once," Charli said.

"What?" Bunny's breath caught and she leaned so far forward on her stool she almost slid off.

"Going twice." Charli paused. "They're a steal at twelve hundred dollars. Come on ladies, won't one of you bid thirteen hundred?"

Bunny's hand shook, her grip clenching on the paddle. Before she could analyze her actions, she raised her paddle.

"Is that Bunny Leigh back there near the bar?" Charli shielded her eyes from the glare of the stage lights. "Y'all gonna let Temptation's best florist go home with the two most drool-worthy men in the county?"

Cory and Jack stared across the room, straight at Bunny, both smiling.

Her pulse accelerated until she thought for certain her heart would jump right out of her chest. Her gaze panned the room, praying someone else would raise a paddle quickly before she bought the cowboy and the cop.

Charli grinned, and before anyone else could get a paddle above shoulder-high, she pounded her gavel on the podium and shouted, "Sold!"

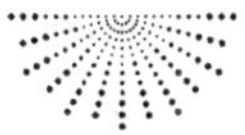

CHAPTER TWO

*H*er heart screeched to a stop and Bunny nearly fell out of her seat.

Audrey pounded her back, smiling from ear to ear. "I knew you had it in you."

"Oh, my gosh." Bunny pressed a hand to her forehead. "What have I done?"

"You've bought a date with two of the hottest men in the tri-county area." Audrey wasn't helping. Her joy didn't make Bunny feel any better about having spent a good portion of her savings account on a single date.

"I can't afford thirteen hundred dollars. I have to pay the wholesaler on Monday."

Audrey hugged her. "I told you, I'd give you half. I wanted to contribute to the auction, and this is perfect. And I don't have to explain myself to Jackson. You get to go home with the goods, not me." She danced away, calling over her shoulder, "I'll be right back with a check for my half."

Okay, six hundred and fifty dollars was better, but still…what was she going to do on a date with two men?

One by one, women paraded by her, some glaring, others congratulating her on her purchase.

Mona, Bunny's hairstylist and best friend, snuck in for a hug. "Wow, I wish I had that kind of money. Those two are priceless. I can't wait to hear all about the date at your next hair appointment. And please, don't scrimp on any of the details. That Cory has the moves. And Jack…" Mona pressed a hand to her chest. "Love a man in uniform." She hugged Bunny again. "I'd give my right arm to trade places with you."

Bunny opened her mouth to say she could, but her gaze caught Cory's as he crossed the room, still in his stripper outfit of chaps, G-string and vest. Every woman he passed pinched his ass.

By the time he reached her, he was rubbing his bare ass, grimacing. "I'm not going to be much to look at with all the bruises I collected running the gauntlet." He laughed and pulled Bunny into his arms. "Thanks."

"For w-what?" Bunny stammered. "You're the one who volunteered for this gig. I should be thanking you and Jack. Look, Cory, as for the date, you don't have to—"

He grabbed her waist and swung her around. "Honey Bunny, you're gonna love what we've got planned for you." Cory slowed to a stop and set her down, holding her at arms' length. "We'll have double the fun."

Stunned by the bare-chested hug, Bunny struggled to breathe and to recall what she'd been about to say.

Jack joined Cory, still shirtless and gorgeous. "Feels good to play the bad-boy cop." He picked her up and kissed her soundly on the lips. "So when's the big date night?"

Her head spinning, Bunny blinked. "I don't know." She didn't know what had come over her, or Jack and Cory, for that matter. Why were they interested in her now? Why did she think she could handle two men when she hadn't dated one in years? Her gaze landed on Cory's rock-hard chest. Holy hell, he was even more attractive with his shirt off. Feeling like a cougar, Bunny forced her attention to Jack, whose dark good looks were completely opposite Cory's blond sexiness. Dating both men could prove to be a minefield of possibilities that might blow up in her face every step of the way. Question was, would it be a good explosion or a bad one?

Cory was everything her ex wasn't, and five years too young for her. If she was smart, she'd concentrate on Jack to keep from cradle-robbing the youngster. Not that Cory looked anything like a boy. Broad shoulders, tight abs and that huge black-clad bulge…

Bunny's thighs clenched and her pussy heated. The only way this date would work was if she kept her head together and her hands off.

"We need time to make the arrangements," Cory said.

Time was good. Bunny opened her mouth to suggest a year, instead she asked, "What arrangements? It's just a date."

"You know—reservations, renting tuxedoes, ordering flowers…" Cory counted them off on his fingers. "How about tomorrow night?"

Jack grinned. "No rush."

Cory threw back his shoulders. "It won't be just *any* date. Since it's you, I have something even more exciting planned."

Bunny's heartbeat kicked up a notch at Cory's air of steely confidence and the wicked gleam in his blue eyes. If she didn't know better, she'd guess Cory was a lot older than his twenty-one years.

"You guys don't have to go to a lot of trouble. Pizza and a movie would be fine by me."

"No pizza." Cory's lips pressed together. "You deserve much better than just pizza."

Bunny crossed her arms. "I'm not into fancy dinners at expensive restaurants."

Cory frowned. "How fancy are you talking?"

"Anything fancier than what we have in Temptation."

Jack laughed. "That narrows it down to PJ's Diner."

His frown deepening, Cory continued, "I wanted to take you out to dinner and dancing."

"That would mean heading all the way into Dallas." Bunny shook her head. "Too far." And if they stayed the night in Dallas, would they share a hotel room?

A tingle of anticipation rippled through her. Two men, one woman and a hotel room? Her breath caught and her palms grew moist. Bunny reminded herself this was only a date, not an all-nighter. Keeping it closer to home would be a better bet.

And safer. From whom? Cory had always been the perfect gentleman when working for her, never making crude comments or moves toward her that could be construed as come-ons. And Jack was a deputy, for goodness sakes. He wouldn't jump her bones. Would he? The thought of either of these men jumping her was ludicrous.

Then why was her pulse pounding through her veins like a base drummer on steroids? Did she actually want them to try something wicked? Was she that brave?

Warmth stole across her body, pooling low in her belly. Man, it had been way too long since she'd had sex with anything but her vibrator. How would it feel to have a man between her legs instead of a battery-powered toy?

Her cheeks heated and she glanced at her hands in her lap to keep from revealing her thoughts. "I'd prefer to do the date locally." Not to mention the other damper on that thought. "And tomorrow is out. I promised Lacey Lambert I'd go with her to the Temptation Garden Club meeting."

Cory tipped his head, his eyes narrowing, staring at Bunny for an agonizingly long moment before he nodded, his face brightening. "Fair enough. How's Friday?"

Bunny glanced around, searching for an excuse and coming up blank. "I guess Friday's good."

"It's settled then." He gripped her hands. "This is your date, so we'll make it special here in Temptation."

Jack's brows rose. "What do you want me to do?"

"Leave it to me. I have an idea." Cory clapped his hands and grinned.

Jack nodded. "Okay, and Friday night's good. I'm off duty."

Cory continued, "We can iron out the details later."

Bunny's gaze bounced from Cory to Jack and back to Cory, like a spectator at a tennis match. A tinge of irritation flared at the cavalier way they were talking around her, as if she didn't have a say in how their date would go. "If you'll excuse me, I'll go pay out." She slipped off the barstool and left the two men discussing the date the three of them would be going on.

Her knees wobbled as she set off across the floor to pay for her winning bid on the two hottest men in the tri-county area. *Holy rock stars!* She didn't have a clue what to do with two men. Never in her entire life had she even considered going out with two guys at once. Friday night, it would happen.

Charli stood beside the cashier, her eyes wide, her smile growing. She glanced at Bunny. "The Ladies Aide made over ten grand on tonight's auction. That's the most they've ever made at one of these shindigs." Charli slipped an arm around Bunny's shoulder. "And the best part is that you have a date with the hottest duo on the program."

Bunny closed her eyes and reminded herself to breathe. Every time she thought about Cory and Jack, her lungs wouldn't work and that sensitive place between her legs ached in anticipation of Friday night.

She handed over Audrey's check and wrote out another for six hundred and fifty dollars. As she passed it over to the cashier, she wondered yet again what the heck she was doing.

Six hundred and fifty dollars would pay one month's rent on the flower shop. Six hundred and fifty dollars would go a long way toward a nice fat shipment of fresh roses. Six hundred and fifty dollars would make a dent in the eight thousand she still owed Ray for his half of everything she'd built while he'd gone to school. Instead, six hundred and fifty dollars was paying for the most expensive date she'd ever been on.

What did people do on dates these days? When she'd handed over her check, she turned to face the dance floor. Every woman in the place had taken to the wood parquet flooring and was gyrating to the tune of "It's Raining Men."

"Come dance!" Mona waved at her from the edge of the throng.

Still reeling from her spontaneous acquisition, Bunny smiled and shook her head pointing toward the hallway that led to the bathrooms. She didn't have to go, but the crowd, the noise and her insane bid had her heart beating too fast. She had to get away, to get out of the bar. As she pushed through the throng, she spied Cory and Jack ducking through the door behind the bar to the back of the saloon, presumably to change and possibly leave.

She couldn't do it. Those two men were way more than she could handle. Bunny turned to follow, determined to tell the guys never mind, the date was off. She didn't want to go out with either one of them; she wasn't ready. After only two short years since her divorce, Bunny wasn't ready to wade through the swamps of dating.

After bumping into two drunk women and dodging around several others, Bunny finally made it to the doorway leading backstage. She glanced around, looking for Greta Sue, the bouncer. When she spied the big woman across the floor near the exit, Bunny sighed. Too bad Greta wasn't there to glare down at her and tell her the back rooms were off limits to customers. The bouncer's interference would have saved Bunny from the additional embarrassment of a face-to-face meeting with the cowboy and the cop. She could have had Greta Sue give them a note, telling them she'd changed her mind. The money was paid. That was all that mattered. She didn't have to follow through on the date.

Bunny slipped through the doorway into the back behind the bar, passing the storeroom where extra boxes of booze were stacked.

Audrey was inside, reaching for a box on an upper shelf. A man snagged her around the waist and pulled her back. "Jackson, stop!" The saloon owner giggled and turned into the man's arms.

Jackson shifted into view. Before Bunny could look away, Jackson's hands slid up Audrey's shirt.

Bunny gasped softly, averted her eyes and rushed into the costume room.

Jack and Cory stood with their backs toward the door.

Cory had taken off the leather vest, boots and chaps and stood in nothing but the black G-string. He was holding his blue jeans in his hands. It wasn't the jeans that captured Bunny's attention and breath.

It was the smooth tanned perfection of Cory's ass.

Jack was slipping his uniform shirt back on and buttoning. "I have to get back out there."

"Talk when you get home?"

"I'll be working late helping Audrey clean up, then I have to report into the station early in the morning."

"How's coffee at the diner at around ten-thirty sound?" Cory stepped into his jeans and pulled them up over that tight set of glutes.

"Good. I'll double check the schedule and make sure no one penciled me in for the night shift on Friday."

"I'm just glad it was Bunny who got us."

"Me too. Some of those women out there were pretty intense."

"Downright scary."

"Practically rabid, if you ask me." Jack chuckled. "Best part is, imagining all the sexy things we can do with Bunny."

Bunny clapped a hand to her lips to keep from gasping out loud. Sexy things? Like what?

"You and me both. Good thing we can agree on that." Cory laughed and turned toward Jack, his gaze tracking to Bunny. He smiled, his hands pausing at the bottom of his zipper. "We have company."

Jack spun, his eyes wide. When he spotted Bunny, he smiled. "Speak of the devil."

Heat climbed up Bunny's neck into her cheeks. She felt like she'd been caught peeking into the boys' locker room in high school.

"Let me just say thanks again for bidding on us." Jack finished the last button on his shirt and tucked the tails into his uniform trousers. "I didn't know what to expect when I volunteered for this."

"You did great. Taking off your shirt." Cory gave Jack a thumbs-up. "Nothing like showing a little skin to get the bidding up."

Bunny couldn't agree more. The amount of skin Jack had been showing had sent her head into a whirl she had yet to fight her way out of. She struggled to remember what she'd come back there to tell them.

Shouts rose from the ladies in the saloon.

Jack glanced toward the sound and sighed. "I'd love to stay and give you a good sample of what to expect on our date, but duty calls." He nodded to Cory. "See you tomorrow at the diner."

Cory nodded. "Nine."

"You're on." Jack gripped Bunny's shoulders and kissed her soundly, then hurried back into the saloon.

Which left Bunny alone with Cory, her lips burning from Jack's kiss.

"Did you want to get a head start on what it will be

like to go out with the two of us?" Cory winked. He'd left his zipper down, the bulge of his black-clad package shining through his pre-washed, denim jeans. He closed the distance between himself and Bunny. "Why are you frowning? We won't bite." He waggled his brows. "Unless you want us to."

"That's it. I'm not ready for the two of you to get into my panties."

Cory grinned. "So, you've been thinking about that too?"

Her face heated and she wished she could take the part about the panties back. "It's just a date. No funny business."

He raised his hand. "Promise…unless you want funny business." He gripped her hand. "Funny business can be pretty great with Jack and me."

She broke free of his grip and turned her back on him. "I haven't been on a date since high school. That's almost ten years ago. Frankly, I came back here to call it off. I paid my bid, but I don't want to go through with this date."

Strong arms slipped around her from behind and pulled her against him. "We promise to be gentle," Cory whispered against her ear, his minty fresh breath stirring the loose tendrils against her cheek.

Bunny inhaled and closed her eyes, pretending this rock-hard man was her equal in age, and she'd never been used and dumped by her worthless ex-husband. If everything was perfect in a perfect world, she might consider going out with Cory and maybe even making love to him.

She inhaled, her senses stormed by the scent of his aftershave.

"You're a beautiful woman, Bunny. Let us show you a good time."

"I should go out with men my own age," she whispered.

"Is that the only thing that's got your pretty panties in a wad?" Cory chuckled. "As a stripper, I've seen it all and matured much faster than anyone else my age." He turned her in his arms and smiled down into her eyes. "Unlike my peers, I know what I want, and I'm not afraid to go after it." He tipped her chin and bent until his lips hovered over hers. "And I want you."

Mesmerized by the clear Texas-sky blue of his eyes, Bunny couldn't look away. Cory was so different from her ex. He was taller, stronger and sunny. Even with a serious expression on his face, the man made the room brighter.

His hands tightened on her arms. "You're so tense. How long has it been since you let loose and laughed?"

She shrugged. Come to think of it, she'd been in a slump since she'd signed the divorce papers two years ago. Still…

Cory shook his head. "Don't second guess your-self. Just feel. Let me show you how to have fun again." His lips descended and claimed hers in a tender kiss.

For a moment Bunny thought she could handle it. She told herself the kiss was one exchanged by friends. Soft, easy, meaning nothing but mutual admiration.

Cory increased the pressure on her mouth, his tongue darting out, urging her to open to his assault.

Bunny's body betrayed her. Heat flamed at her core, spreading like a wildfire throughout her body. One moment she was kissing a young man who was still in middle school when she'd gotten married. The next, she'd forgotten where she was, her total focus on what those lips were doing to her and where his hands were leading.

Cory's fingers traveled down her arms, skimming the curve of her waist and stopping to cup her ass. He lifted her, wrapping her legs around him. Her jean skirt inched up around her hips as he backed her against the nearest wall. He broke the kiss long enough to say, "You're so very beautiful." Then his mouth left a trail of kisses and tender nips along her jaw line and down the long column of her neck.

Lost to reason, Bunny tipped her head to the side, allowing Cory more access to the curve at the base of her throat. She threaded her fingers through his hair, urging him closer. His member pressed into the V of her crotch, nudging her entrance through the thin silk of her panties.

Bunny moaned as her pussy creamed. Being held like this, kissed and touched by a man with big, callused hands and broad, muscular shoulders was so much better than the cold, lifeless coaxing of her vibrator. This was what Audrey had been talking about—what Bunny had forgotten from the first forays into intense teenaged sex, when her hormones were raging and she couldn't get enough.

Cory balanced her with one hand and reached between them to peel her panties to the side and slide a finger along that sensitive nubbin of throbbing nerves.

Bunny gasped. Her breath caught and held, waiting for the next stroke.

He touched her again, this time slow and steady, sliding downward to the opening of her pussy, slick with fresh juices.

"Oh, sweet Jesus, you're wet." He kissed her, his tongue thrusting past her teeth, sliding alongside hers.

Past coherent thought, Bunny squirmed against the finger flicking her clit, wanting more...much more. She wiggled to get closer to the hardness of his cock straining against the slick black fabric of his G-string. Why, oh why was he still wearing clothes?

Footsteps sounded behind them. The steady click of boot heels hitting wood flooring moved closer, piercing the mind-numbing things Cory was doing to Bunny's body.

As she surfaced for air, Bunny opened her eyes and stared across the costume room, straight into Audrey Anderson's smiling face.

Bunny braced her hands on Cory's shoulders. "Stop."

Cory looked up, his blue eyes glazed with passion. "Stop?"

Audrey raised her hands. "Don't stop on my

account." She chuckled. "I was enjoying the show. It's not often I get to watch."

Cory shook his head, joining Audrey's chuckle with one of his own. "Anyone ever tell you that you have lousy timing?" He let Bunny's legs slide down his until her feet touched the ground.

Her cheeks flaming, Bunny straightened her skirt and pulled her shirt and bra down over her breasts. When had they inched upward? Mortified and unable to face Audrey, she muttered something about needing to get up to work the next morning and hit the back exit door.

Not until she stood in the rear parking lot, inhaling the fresh Texas night air, did she stop to think.

Holy hell.

She was in a lot of trouble if that's what Cory expected to happen on date night. And then it would be two men. Bunny had never considered anything quite so naughty.

Holy hell.

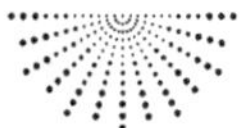

ona showed up at the door to Sweet Temptations Flower Shop as soon as Bunny flipped the Closed sign to Open. She pushed through the door, the bell overhead ringing loudly.

Bunny pressed fingers to her temples and moaned, wishing she'd removed the bell long ago. On most days, she was happy Mona's Shear Safari Hair Salon was right next door to her flower shop.

Not today.

"Nice dress." Mona followed Bunny to the room in the rear of the shop. "Is it new?"

"This ol' thing." Bunny shook her head. "Ran out of clean jeans." She hadn't really, but something about what happened the night before made her a little more selective of her clothing today. In case someone —or two someones—happened to stop in.

"Spill, girlfriend. Tell me all," Mona demanded.

Bunny turned away, her cheeks heating. "Nothing to tell."

"Oh, no you don't." Mona jumped in front of her. "What made you take such a wild step last night? I was under the impression you'd given up on men." She glanced at her fingers. "What's it been, two years since jerk-face Ray walked out on you for an airheaded dental assistant?"

"Two years yesterday." Bunny heaved a sigh. "And I don't know what came over me last night. Must have been the second beer." Heck, she hadn't even had two sips out of the second mug before she'd flipped her paddle and bought two incredibly sexy men. Or at least a date with them. Maybe it had something to do with the anniversary of her divorce. Or maybe it was her ex's upcoming wedding or the rut she'd dug herself into that had sent her flying over the edge. Whatever it was, the deed was done. She'd bought the date.

She slumped onto the stool at her worktable. "I'm already regretting it," she lied. After what happened with Cory in the costume room, Bunny couldn't stop thinking about what might happen Friday night with both Cory and Jack. For the first time in months, she looked forward to something besides getting up and going to work. Bunny lifted a rose and twirled it between her fingers. Ever since last night, she hadn't been able to sit still. Her entire body was twitchy, needy, wanting something, and not sure she could wait until Friday to get it.

Mona pried the long stem from her fingers and laid it on the counter. "It's about time you had a little romance in your life."

Bunny snorted. "What are you talking about? I'm surrounded by romance." She waved her hand at the flower arrangements set in neat little groups, ready to be delivered that day.

"You're surrounded by other people's romances. You deserve a little romance of your own." Mona frowned. "When was the last time someone sent *you* flowers or paid *you* a compliment?"

Compliments? Her cheeks heated as she recalled Jack's and Cory's words last night. She had no intention of telling Mona. Not now. Not when this was all so new and she didn't know where it was going.

Mona snapped her fingers in front of Bunny's face. "Earth to Bunny. Well?"

Bunny blinked, coming back to the flower shop and Mona. "Well what?"

"When was the last time anyone gave you flowers?" Mona demanded.

"Flowers?" Bunny's brows furrowed. "Not since my wedding, and I paid for those myself."

Mona propped her fists on her hips. "Wow, your love life is worse than mine."

Bunny jumped on her comment, hoping for a reprieve on airing her own pathetic shortcomings in the love department. "Speaking of which, when was the last time someone sent *you* flowers? And when was the last time *you* went on a date? Seems to me you were the one all turned off by guys. What was it you said…?" Bunny tapped her chin. "Oh, yeah. You were considering being a lesbian."

Mona's lips pressed together. "And if I recall, you turned me down." She shrugged. "I can't even get a date with a girl."

The tension leached out of Bunny's shoulders, and she hugged Mona. "We really are pathetic, you know."

"At least you have a date." Mona hugged her. "Don't back out on it. Even if it doesn't come to anything, at least you're getting out there. Maybe this date will encourage you to be open to others. The added bonus is that I get to live vicariously through you."

"That might prove disappointing." Bunny lifted the rose again and handed it to Mona. "When are you going to get back in the saddle?"

Mona let out a long sigh. "I don't know. But after seeing all those guys last night without their shirts on… Well let's just say my vibrator got a workout and it wasn't nearly as satisfying as I'd hoped."

Exactly Bunny's sentiment. After Cory had touched her…there…she hadn't been the same. Even the memory of his fingers stroking her set her off on the road to orgasm.

The bell over the front door jangled. Tom Weinfelt entered, there to pick up the spray of daisies he'd requested for his wife's grave. The ninety-three-year-old man shuffled through the door. "Mornin', Ms. Bunny."

"Mornin', Mr. Weinfelt."

Mona jumped, her gaze shooting to the clock over the worktable. "You have a customer, and I have to go. Mrs. Franzten's cut-and-'do won't wait. Have lunch with me?"

"Can't. I have a lot of deliveries to make today, and I need to start arranging flowers for a wedding."

"Oh, yeah, your jerk-face ex and his bubble-headed bride." Mona shook her head. "I still can't believe you agreed to do it."

Bunny sighed. "I still owe him eight grand. I had to do it in trade for some of my debt."

"Slime ball. You put him through dental school. You don't own him a thing."

"Yeah, but it's a community property state. He got half of everything. Including my business. And until I get enough to pay him off…"

Mona glared. "Be cheaper to hire a hit man."

Bunny smiled. "I think of it as proving to myself I'm over him and don't care. Although a drink at the Ugly Stick after the wedding would be fabulous."

"You're on." Mona left, the bell over the door ringing loudly in her wake.

A few minutes later, Mr. Weinfelt had gone with his daisies to pay his respect to his dearly departed wife. The old man smiled at her, but the smile didn't reach his sad eyes. He'd loved his wife Nora so much. When she'd been on her deathbed, he'd promised to bring her daisies every week for the rest of his life.

When Bunny had married Ray, she'd believed their love was strong enough to last a lifetime and dreamed they'd grow old together, like Tom and Nora Weinfelt. A lump rose in her throat as she pictured Mr. Weinfelt laying the daisies on Nora's grave. Bunny pushed her hair back from her forehead and closed her eyes. Deep in her heart, she wanted to believe in that dream. She opened her eyes to the sun shining through the front window and went back to work.

Settling in behind her workbench, she let her mind drift back to the two men in the costume room and all the deliciously naughty things she could imagine doing with them. Never in her life had she considered being with more than one man. Hell, she'd married right out of high school, so her sleeping around days had been over before they started. She'd married her high school sweetheart and the only man she'd ever made love to.

Now she was arranging flowers for that man's wedding.

She smiled. The promise of her date with Cory and Jack was so tantalizing that even thinking about her ex couldn't put a damper on it. Her belly tightened and a soft throbbing ache developed between her legs. Jack and Cory had stirred up a tempest inside her, and there appeared to be only one way to exorcise it.

JACK STOPPED by the sheriff's office early Thursday morning and checked the schedule. As he'd expected, he was off Friday night.

Deputy Mitch Cramer stepped up beside Jack and

tapped the schedule posted on the wall. "Wanna fill in for me tomorrow night?"

"No."

"Damn, Jack." Cramer stepped back, a frown denting his forehead. "You could have at least hesitated a little. You're usually good in a pinch."

A smile lifted the corners of Jack's lips. "Got plans."

Cramer's frown deepened. "Plans, huh?" Then his brows rose and he gave a bark of laughter. "That's right. Last night was the Cowboy Auction. Who got the winning bid? Some old lady from the Garden Club?" He laughed again. "What was it like to be viewed like a horse at the livestock sale?"

Jack didn't bother to answer. He settled his cowboy hat on his head, left the sheriff's station and drove his truck to the edge of town. Two miles out, he turned onto Shady Lane and drove beneath the wrought-iron arches of Shady Grove Cemetery. Jack parked beside a vintage Crown Victoria, beneath the hundred-year-old white oak tree.

For a long moment, he sat staring across the neat row of headstones. At first, he didn't see anyone else. Then Mr. Weinfelt straightened and wiped a shaking hand across his eyes as he stared down at a grave. After a few more minutes, the old man looked toward where Jack had parked. He bent one last time, then stood as straight as his hunched figure could and shuffled toward Jack.

Jack climbed from the truck and met Mr. Weinfelt at the front of his car, removing his hat from his head out of respect for the ninety-three-year-old. "Mornin', Mr. Weinfelt."

"Mornin', Jack." The older man held out his hand.

Jack clasped the man's hand and shook it, the older man's parchment skin cool to his touch. "Bring Ms. Nora her daisies?"

Mr. Weinfelt nodded toward the sun halfway up the eastern sky. "Nora loved sunny days and daisies. Couldn't disappoint her." He held out his other hand with a single daisy in it. "Thought you might like this one for Stacy."

Jack took the daisy and smiled at Mr. Wienfelt, his heart squeezing in his chest. "Sure Nora won't mind?"

"She always liked little Stacy." He smiled and climbed into his Crown Victoria, driving away in a puff of dust.

Jack plunked his cowboy hat on his head and wove through the headstones, until he reached hers. "Hi, Stacy." He squatted beside the marker and laid the single daisy at the base of the granite. "Remember how you always got jealous when I looked at another girl? Well, I've been doin' a lot of thinkin' lately and I know you'd want me to be happy, no matter what. You always had such a big heart and, if you could, you'd tell me it was time to move on." He scraped his hat off and twirled it slowly between his fingers. "Hope you don't mind, but me and Cory kinda like Ms. Bunny Leigh from the flower shop, and we'd like to date her." He paused, closed his eyes and listened for a sound, a sign, anything that he could construe as a response.

Nothing stirred, not a breeze, bird or insect made a sound. Even the traffic on the highway seemed to have disappeared. Who was he trying to kid? Stacy had been dead for three years. She couldn't hear him all the way up there in heaven. He kissed his fingertips and touched the name engraved on the stone. "I'll always love you, sweetheart. But I have room in my heart to love again. I just know it."

Jack pushed to his feet, settled his cowboy hat on his head and stared across the central Texas horizon —the rolling hills, the huge, pale blue sky and the soft green pastures stretching away from the cemetery. Stacy had loved the Texas sunshine, just like Nora Wienfelt. The warmth of the sun on his back felt like a caress. Almost as if Stacy was smiling down at him, touching his back with a soft hand, urging him to find another love to fill the lonely hours.

As he walked toward the truck, the soft coo of a dove sounded from the big oak tree. Jack tipped his hat back and looked up in time to see a gray dove take off, its wings spread in flight.

The bird dipped low over his head and winged away into the brightness of the morning sunshine.

Yup, it had to be a sign. With a lighter heart, Jack climbed into his truck and headed to town. After he and Cory talked through the details, they'd start courting Bunny. And with Stacy's blessing, they couldn't lose.

"So it's agreed?" Cory leaned back in the booth at

PJ's Diner at ten past eleven o'clock that morning. "The date is set. It'll be the both of us, and we'll behave like gentlemen. No expectations of anything afterward?"

Jack sighed. "I had hoped for more. I hadn't realized just how obsessed I was with her until I counted the number of bud vases in my closets. Do you realize I've been in that flower shop once a week for six months? I have twenty-six vases taking up room at the house."

"Take them back to Bunny. She could use them for your next twenty-six purchases."

"I can't do that. Then she'll know I wasn't buying them for my mother."

Cory shook his head. Jack had a heart as big as his shoe size. "Well, don't think I'm going to let you win her over all to yourself. I've been delivering flowers for her for the past three months, even though I don't need the money."

"You know? We're pretty darned pathetic if you ask me. Why the hell have we been beatin' around the bush when we could have fessed up and been datin' her all along?"

"I didn't want to commit to anything until I finished my undergrad degree And with med school looming, I'm still straddlin' the fence. She put her ex through dental school. I wouldn't blame her if she ran screaming from a relationship with me, because I'm going to be gone to school in Dallas all week, every week for four years."

"Yeah, you got it rough." Jack's lips quirked upward

on the sides. "Which should make her decision easy. She'll choose me."

"Over my dead body. I thought of dating her first."

"I've been courtin' her in my own way for six months."

"Buying flowers for your mother?" Cory snorted. "Look, buddy, we've already agreed to *share* Bunny. Stick to the plan. We need to get her used to the idea of having both of us. Which means we need to let her see us separately, get to know each of us individually, and then ease her into the idea of both of us."

"I'll take lunch today, since I'm working the night shift," Jack jumped in.

"Okay. Which means I gotta coax an invite to the Temptation Garden Club meeting tonight." Cory let out a long breath. "Joy." He pushed back from the table. "Between now and then, I need to get back to my computer. The stock market is supposed to be falling today. I want to get in on some good stock sales." He planned on doing just that...after he stopped in the flower shop to see Bunny.

"Yeah. I need to check on some construction supplies for the house." Jack tossed bills on the table and stood. "Guess I'll see you later."

Cory pushed through the door and turned left.

"Hey, isn't your truck parked over there?" Jack pointed to the right.

With a sigh, Cory realized he wasn't going to get by with a lie. "I thought I'd stop by and see Bunny first."

"Not before me, you aren't." Jack let go of the door

and stepped out smartly, heading straight for the Sweet Temptations Flower Shop.

Cory tore out after him, running to catch up and overtake the big cop. By the time they reached the shop, they were sprinting to the finish line.

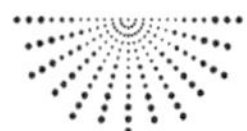

The bell in the front of the shop rang, startling Bunny out of her naughty dreams. "I'll be with you in a minute," she called out.

She shoved a long-stemmed, pink rose into the middle of an elaborate centerpiece and gave the arrangement a brief once-over before stepping through the door to the shop.

"Good morning, beautiful," two deep voices said in unison, albeit in a rush.

Bunny jerked to a stop, her heart leaping into her throat as she stared at the two men at the root of her wicked thoughts. She blinked twice, afraid her over-active imagination had conjured them. "What are you doing here?"

Cory stepped forward and took her hand, drawing her into his arms. "We wanted to make sure you weren't thinkin' of backin' out on our date." He held her in his strong embrace, pressed tightly against his hips, his thick ridge nudging her belly. He bent and touched his lips to hers in a feather-light kiss. "Did you miss us?"

Her pulse pounded and heat suffused her cheeks. Even if she'd wanted to lie and tell him no, her face would have told him the truth. And his arms were so strong, so muscular...

"Hey, move over and let me in on some of that." Jack nudged Cory's shoulder.

Cory growled, the sound more playful than angry. "If you weren't my friend..."

"Yeah, yeah..." Jack wedged himself between Cory and Bunny, sliding his hands down her arms over her hips to the backs of her thighs. "I'm sorry I couldn't stay around last night to give you a taste of what we had in mind. From what Audrey said, Cory dished out a sample of his own. I'm up for sharin' but that doesn't mean I'm not going to show you the better deal you'll get from me." He lifted her, wrapping her legs around his waist.

Bunny squealed, unprepared for his actions. No one had ever come on to her like this in broad daylight. In her flower shop, no less. Her heart skittered and she clung to his shoulders, too shocked and titillated to utter a protest.

"Hey," Cory grumbled. "A sample, buddy, not the full enchilada."

"That's right." Jack walked with her toward the back of the shop. "You can stay here or join us."

Cory followed.

Heat pulsed in waves over Bunny's body as Jack

stopped beside her workbench, next to the huge centerpiece she'd been arranging.

Jack nodded toward the display. "That for Ray and Chrissy's wedding?"

Bunny nodded.

A grin spread over Jack's face. "Then let's make sure we give it the finishing touch."

"What do you mean?" Bunny asked, her voice breathy, her pussy pressed against the bulge of Jack's fly.

He nodded to Cory. "You wanna take the stool?"

"You bet." Cory pulled out a stool and sat, then patted his thighs.

Jack settled Bunny in Cory's lap, her back leaning against the blond's chest.

"What are you doing?" she asked.

"Just say the word, and we'll stop," Jack reassured her. "We want to give you happy thoughts to think as you set up the flowers for your ex's wedding."

Cory spread his big hands over her thighs and parted them.

Bunny gasped. "I don't know about this."

"What's to know?" Jack stepped between Cory's and Bunny's legs and gripped her chin in his palms. "All you have to do is feel."

"Think of last night," Cory whispered against her ear.

A wash of pure heat slid across her skin and centered at her core. With the warmth of Cory's crotch beneath her bottom, the ridge of his cock nudging the crease of her ass, she could barely think.

"Want us to stop?" Cory whispered against her ear.

Here was her chance to put the brakes on.

Should I, or shouldn't I? Oh, what the hell!

Bunny breathed in, then out, and shock her head. "No. Don't stop."

Cory's fingers slid toward her center, making her skin tingle in anticipation.

Jack's hands trailed down the length of her throat and across to push the thin straps of her sundress over her shoulders.

Her fear of being caught by customers soon disappeared when Cory found her entrance, pushing aside the thin silk of her thong panties. Bunny's head fell back against Cory's shoulder. "Do you two do this often?" she whispered.

Jack chuckled as he shoved her dress and bra aside to capture a nipple between his teeth. "Do what?" He rolled the nipple on his tongue and flicked it until it hardened.

Bunny gasped, her chest rising to give him more. "Share."

Cory slid a long, work-roughened finger into her. "Jack and I have been friends for a couple years now." He leaned into her neck and nibbled at her earlobe.

"We've shared once before." Jack switched to the other breast, baring it before taking it fully into his mouth, sucking hard.

Cory slid another magic finger into her cunt. "Have you ever had more than one man at a time?"

Bunny's pussy clenched around Cory's fingers. "No," she gasped.

Jack pulled free of her breast and stared into her eyes. "Does it bother you?"

Bunny moaned, "Yes!"

Cory's fingers paused in mid-stroke.

When he and Jack started to back away, Bunny grabbed him. "It bothers me in a good way. Please…don't stop."

"Aren't you afraid someone will come in?" Cory's breath stirred the hairs around Bunny's neck, sending delicious tingles across her skin.

"Yes!" She didn't know if she was answering his question or responding to the way they made her feel. Who knew it could be this good to have two men?

"Does it make you even more excited?" Jack asked.

Bunny couldn't think past the fingers in her pussy. Ray hadn't believed in foreplay.

These men apparently invented it.

Bunny squirmed against Cory's hardening cock. She wanted more. Jack pushed her bra and dress back in place.

"You're stopping?" Bunny asked, her voice high-pitched.

Cory's chuckle rumbled all the way through Bunny's chest. "Jack won't stop until you tell him, or you come." The gorgeous stripper swirled his two fingers in her wet pussy, then dragged them up to her clit.

Bunny arched her back. "Oh, God. There."

Jack dropped to his knees. "I'll take it from here."

"You got it." Cory slid his hands to her thighs and held them wide.

With the tip of his finger, Jack stroked her from her pussy up to that nubbin of pulsating nerves.

"What are you doing?" Bunny tipped her head forward, her eyes widening as Jack's tongue flicked out and touched her in that most intimate of spots.

"Holy hell." Bunny gasped, falling back against Cory's hard, muscular chest.

Cory chuckled again. "Don't tell me you've never had someone go down on you?"

Caught in a haze of desire so thick she could barely breathe, Bunny could only shake her head as Jack flicked her again. Never in her entire married life had Ray come close to her pussy with his mouth or tongue.

Jack tormented her with one stroke after the next until Bunny grabbed his ears and held him still, her body tightening to the point it exploded over the edge in a starburst of sensations.

Cory held her legs wide while Jack lapped at her clit and pussy, prolonging the orgasm. When Bunny finally went limp, she was grateful Cory held her to keep her from sliding to the floor in a puddle of lust.

Jack straightened, a smile stretching his glistening lips. "That, my dear Bunny, is what you're in store for tomorrow night."

"And more, if you want it." Cory brushed her hair to the side and pressed his lips to her temple. "All you have to do is say the word."

Jack smoothed a hand up to her hip, snagged her panties and slid them down her legs. "I'll keep these until then as a reminder of what's to come and so that you won't forget."

Bunny's back stiffened, and she reached for the panties. "I can't deliver panties without flowers."

Cory laughed out loud. "I hope not."

Bunny slid off his legs, her knees threatening to buckle as her feet hit the floor. "You know what I meant." She straightened her dress and pushed her fingers through her hair, before holding out her hand. "Give them to me."

Jack tossed them to Cory, who stuffed them into his pocket, shaking his head. "Ask me for them tonight, and I'll consider returning them."

"But I won't see you tonight," Bunny wailed.

The bell in the front of the shop rang loudly.

Heat rose up Bunny's cheeks at the thought of waiting on a customer when she wasn't wearing panties.

Jack and Cory headed through the door, leaving her to follow.

"Is Bunny here?" A voice Bunny recognized called out, sending a lump of lead to the pit of her belly.

Bunny stepped out of the workroom, too conscious of her lack of panties to think straight. She forced a cool smile to her face and pushed between Jack and Cory.

The two men she'd won at the auction stuck to her like glue, refusing to move far enough away for Bunny to make sense of her whirling thoughts.

"How can I help you?" Bunny managed.

Chrissy Adley stepped out from behind Ray and

gave her a weak smile. Her pale blond hair was swept back in a ponytail, making her look even younger than her twenty-three years. She was beautiful with her clear, blue eyes and innocence. Bunny could understand what Ray had seen in her. "We came by to double check on the flowers for the wedding."

Jack nodded toward Ray. "This your ex?"

Bunny nodded. "Ray, Chrissy, this is Jack and Cory, my..." She stumbled, not sure what to call the men flanking her who'd just given her a top-notch orgasm in the back room. Her cheeks flamed as the pause lengthened.

"Lovers," Jack finished for her, slipping an arm around her shoulder.

Cory's arm rose around her waist, his hand sliding down over her near-naked fanny, reminding her that all that stood between his hand and her ass was the thin fabric of her sundress.

"Congratulations on your upcoming nuptials," Cory addressed Chrissy.

She smiled, her gaze darting to Bunny. "Er...thank you."

Bunny almost felt sorry for the girl. She was in for years of boring sex with Ray. "I just finished the centerpiece for the head table, and the rest will be complete and delivered by noon tomorrow."

"Oh, good," Chrissy gushed. "I was afraid..."

Bunny's brows rose. "Afraid?"

Chrissy blushed. "Nothing."

"She was afraid you'd harbor a grudge toward her," Ray interjected, slipping an arm around his fiancée. "I

told her that was silly. You always take business seriously." He snorted. "Or, I *thought* you did."

Bunny smiled though gritted teeth. "You're absolutely right…when it comes to my business, I take it
seriously." Or as seriously as she could with a naked
bottom.

"See?" Ray turned to Chrissy. "The wedding will be
fine. Can we go now?"

Chrissy smiled at Bunny. "No hard feelings?"

"Toward you?" Bunny shook her head and smiled
at the younger woman, understanding more what
Cory had meant when he said women his own age
were clueless. "I don't hold a grudge against you,
Chrissy." *Just that dumbass who stole half my business.*

Jack snorted, a fleeting grin spreading across his
face, before he adopted his poker face again.

Cory's blue-eyed gaze focused on Ray and he
stuck out a hand. "Just wanted to say thanks."

Ray grasped Cory's hand, his eyes narrowing.
"For what?"

With his other arm, Cory pulled Bunny snugly
against him. "For leavin' Bunny. She deserves better."

Chrissy gasped, and Ray dropped Cory's hand and
glared. "How dare you?"

Cory shrugged. "Just callin' it as I see it."

Ray and Chrissy left the shop in a hurry, without
saying goodbye, the doorbell jingling merrily in their
shocked wake.

Even as the door closed, Jack and Cory were
laughing.

Bunny couldn't be mad at them, not with the

aftershocks of her orgasm still rippling through her. "If you two are through disrupting my work, could you leave?"

Jack saluted. "Yes, ma'am." He grabbed her and bent her over in a long, romantic kiss, then set her on her feet. "Be thinkin' of me."

Bunny smoothed her hair and struggled to regain her equilibrium when Cory caught her and crushed her to him.

"And be thinkin' of me." His hand slid down to her bottom, lifting the hem of her dress to cup her naked ass.

"Guys, I've got work to do," she said, her voice breathless, her nerves on fire.

Cory nodded and leaned close, his eyelids slanting low. "We dare you to go commando all day." He winked, kissed her and said, "It'll get you in the mood for later." With that parting comment, the two men left.

Bunny stared after them until they disappeared down the street.

Later? What did they mean later?

At half past twelve, Bunny still hadn't finished loading her delivery van with the morning's collection of flowers to be delivered. If she didn't get a move on, she'd be arranging tomorrow's bouquets well into the evening and miss the Temptation Garden Club meeting with Lacey. Though Lacey had already proved her point with the snooty old guard of the club at the last meeting, she could still do with a friend to watch her back and be there for moral support.

Why Lacey went to the meetings was beyond Bunny. After the old biddies treated Lacey so badly when she got her divorce, Bunny couldn't understand why Lacey ever went back. Then again, since she and Nick McBride had hooked up and moved into his big new house, Lacey had taken a whole new interest in gardening to establish the flowerbeds around her new place. She'd never been happier.

Bunny sighed and stared around her work area without seeing it. Lacey and Nick were so silly in love it made her envious. As soon as that thought popped into her head, more images of Cory and Jack sizzled through her mind, reminding her that she was still panty-less. Her pussy clenched, and she reached beneath her dress, pressing against her mound to ease the ache. What would it be like to be loved? Really loved. Ray had never been that sensitive to her needs. He'd never been interested in showing her new and different ways to quench her desires. Get in, get out and get back to his television program was all he'd been interested in.

Oh, but Cory and Jack… Now those two had it down pat.

Bunny paused in the back room of her shop, her fingers gliding over her mound, pushing through the soft hairs to part her folds. As she touched her clit, she moaned, a spark of electricity running from that point throughout her body, sending tingling sensations that raised gooseflesh on her skin.

With a ton of work waiting for her, she hesitated, then flicked her clit again, tapping it with the tip of one fingernail.

Her belly clenched and her pussy creamed. "Oh, my." She glanced through the doorway to the front of the shop, checking to make sure no one lurked out there who might catch her pleasuring herself. Then she slipped her hand lower over her mons and buried her finger in her wet pussy, dipping it in and out of her own juices.

She leaned her butt against her worktable and spread her legs wider, lifting her dress out of the way so that she could watch as she touched herself.

A nervous giggle rose up her throat. Who would have thought Bunny Leigh would be masturbating in the back of her flower shop? Wouldn't her customers be appalled? The incredible naughtiness should have made her stop. Instead, it gave her a thrill of excitement, and she pressed on. With one hand, she parted her folds, with the other she slathered her clit with her pussy cream and swirled it around and around in slow, sensuous strokes. Her head dropped back and she closed her eyes as exquisite sensations rippled through her.

She rocked her pelvis to the rhythm of her strokes, her breathing becoming more labored, interspersed with deep, guttural moans. 'Yes. There. Oh, yes," she muttered.

As her muscles tensed, her buttocks clenched and

she paused in mid-stroke, the sweet torture so intense she rode it through, catapulting over the edge. So sweet, so satisfying…but not enough. She wanted more. A hard, rigid cock buried to the balls inside her, fucking her until she came again. She clumped her fingers together and shoved them into her vagina, pushing hard. They weren't long enough and they weren't attached to a handsome, living, breathing cop or pre-med cowboy. One dark and brooding, the other blond and gorgeous.

She thrust deeper, her thumb finding her clit, rubbing to start the rise back to orgasm all over again. "Almost there." Her breath hitched and she cried out as she did it again, launching herself over the edge a second time.

The bell over the front door jangled, ripping through her mindless masturbation. She yanked her fingers from her crotch and hurried to her sink in the back. "Be right with you," she called out.

As she washed the evidence of her dirty deeds from her hands, she breathed in and out to steady her racing heart.

Arms slipped around her and pulled her against a muscled chest.

Bunny stiffened.

"Thinking about me?" a deep voice said behind her, the sound rumbling through her back into her chest.

All her muscles turned to jelly, and she leaned into him. Not only had she been thinking about him, she'd been masturbating to the images in her mind of him and Cory pleasuring her earlier that morning. "How's a girl to get anything done if you two keep turning up?" It wasn't much of a protest delivered on a breathy whisper.

"I came to take you out to lunch."

She sighed, remembering all the flowers waiting in her van, possibly wilting in the noon sun. "Oh, Jack, I can't." Bunny turned in his arms. "I have so many deliveries to make, I can't even stop for a bite."

"Then let me help." His hands slid down her arms to her waist and he pulled her to him, the ridge of his fly pressing into her belly, reminding her of what she'd just done and how much she wanted him.

As much as she wanted to skip deliveries and remain in her workroom, fucking the cop, she couldn't. Duty called. She wouldn't stay in business long if she didn't delivery flowers when she promised. "I can't ask you to do that."

He tipped her chin up and gazed into her eyes. "I'm offering on a purely selfish basis. The sooner you deliver, the sooner you can take a break for lunch. Now, are you going to argue or are we going to deliver?" His hand slipped lower to cup her ass.

She brushed his hand away, her cheeks burning. "I haven't had time to get a fresh pair, in case you're wondering." And she didn't want him to know just how turned on she was, which would be apparent if he got anywhere close to her drenched pussy. What would he think if he knew she'd just come in her workroom? Would he want to stay and go for round two?

Her heart fluttered. God, she wanted him. The sun shining through the front window of the shop served as a reminder that she had a job to do, and making love in the back of her flower shop wasn't going to get it done. "Okay, then, let's go." She ducked beneath his arm, grabbed a box lined with vases and handed it to him before he could put his arms around her again. Bunny hefted another box of arrangements and hurried toward the front door before she could change her mind. She flipped the Open sign to Closed and held the door for Jack.

He winked at her as he passed.

Her heart racing, Bunny locked the front door and climbed into the driver's seat of her van, while Jack settled into the passenger seat. "I thought you had to work today."

"Tonight. Got the four to midnight shift."

"Shouldn't you be resting?"

"I'm good." He grinned at her and nodded toward the windshield. "Where to first?"

Bunny drove off, happy to have the help, but nervous the entire time, smoothing the hem of her dress down every time she got out of the van. A pesky Texas breeze picked up, ruffling her skirt with every step she took.

Jack had a perpetual smile on his lips every time his gaze locked in on her legs right below her hem.

Half the time Bunny wanted to slap the lecherous look from his face, the other half of the time, she couldn't hold back the jolt of desire the heat in his eyes inspired. By the time they got to the last order, it was one thirty and, though her stomach growled, she couldn't wait to get back to the shop, take Jack to the back room and rumble.

Mrs. Diffee smiled at Jack as she accepted the huge arrangements she'd ordered for the church. "Jack, honey, when did you start workin' for Ms. Bunny?"

"When I noticed what pretty legs she has." He winked at the older woman and she blushed. "You have a nice day, now, ya hear?"

Mrs. Diffee blushed and waved them away. "Oh, Jack, you're a scamp."

When Bunny climbed back into the van, her heartbeat ratcheted up and settled into overdrive.

"That's it?" Jack looked at the back of van filled with empty boxes and clapped his hands together. "Time for lunch."

Bunny shook her head. "I have to get back to the shop and work on tomorrow's orders or I'll never get done in time to go to the Garden Club meeting."

Jack frowned. "But I wanted to take you on a picnic."

"I'm sorry. I just don't have time." And she really wanted to go with him. She hadn't been on a picnic since she was a little girl and her parents were still alive. "You really didn't have to do all this. The date I won at auction wasn't intended to last a couple days."

"This has nothing to do with the auction. I want to get to know you better." He stared out the front window a little longer, his forehead creased, a shadow passing over his eyes, then his dark brows rose and the sun returned to his face. "Actually, this works out even better. If you can't go on a picnic, I'll bring it to you."

Bunny glanced at him. "What?"

He smiled her way. "Eyes front. Someone's gotta drive this boat, and Wally would like to live another day."

She looked back at the road in time to swerve and miss a golden retriever crossing the pavement. "Whew." With both hands firmly on the steering wheel and her gaze forward, Bunny made the rest of the trip to the shop without incident. Throughout the drive, butterflies batted their wings against the lining of her stomach. What kind of picnic did he have in mind while she worked in the shop?

As soon as they'd unloaded the boxes, Jack left through the front door, calling out over his shoulder, "Don't go anywhere, I'll be right back."

"Like I have time to run away," Bunny muttered.

Jack ducked his head back through the door. "I heard that." He winked and disappeared.

Her heart slowed to normal in the five minutes Jack was gone, jumping back into hyper speed when he pushed through the door, carrying a large basket covered with a checkered blanket. "Remind me to take flowers to PJ."

"Don't forget to take flowers to PJ." Bunny frowned at the huge basket. "Are you planning on feeding an army?"

"No, but I had to have all the fixings to make this right." Jack stepped past her to the workroom beyond. "Don't mind me. I'll just set up while you work."

"Uh, that's my workroom. I have to work in there." Bunny bit back the chuckle rising in her chest. Jack had such an eager look on his face, she couldn't be mad. She went to work arranging her orders across her worktable while Jack laid the checkered blanket across the tile floor.

On it he placed dinner plates, boxes of fried chicken, fresh biscuits and fruit salad. Then he lifted a bottle of wine and two wine glasses from the basket and settled them on the blanket.

Bunny rose from her stool and bent over the basket, peering in. "Did you happen to pack the kitchen sink as well?"

"Nope, but I did remember the candles." He removed two long white candles, stuck them in two sturdy candleholders and lit each. Finally, he sat back and surveyed the spread before opening his arms wide. "Madame, your lunch is served."

Bunny shook her head. "Seriously?"

Jack's happy face faded. "What? Not enough candles? I'll have to have a talk with PJ."

"No, no. This is…" Bunny laughed. "Wonderful."

"Then sit." He patted the ground beside him. "You need to refuel after all that runnin' around. I didn't know being a florist was so exhausting."

She sat with her legs tucked under her, highly aware she was still without underwear. The coarse fabric of the tablecloth brushed against her naked ass, heating her entire body.

"I had PJ open the bottle with a corkscrew." Jack poured a wine glass half full and handed it to Bunny.

Her fingers tingled where his touched hers, reminding her of how they'd felt on the inside of her thighs only that morning. Wow, had it only been that morning?

Jack poured a quarter of a glass for himself.

Bunny tipped her head. "Trying to get me drunk?"

"Not at all. I have to be on duty in a couple hours." He sniffed the wine and sighed. "Wouldn't be good to show up drunk. Besides, I like beer better." He held his glass up to hers.

"What are we drinking to?" she asked, her hand shaking.

"I'm not good at this. What do you suggest?"

Bunny's thoughts couldn't get past the naughty things they could be doing on that blanket. Her mother would be turning over in her grave. She gulped. "You decide."

He nodded and said quietly, "How about sunshine and doves?"

Bunny clinked her glass against his and tipped it to her lips, taking a sip. "Why do I get the feeling sunshine and doves has a deeper meaning?"

He downed his little bit of wine. "Because it does." Jack reached for her hand, removed the glass from it and tugged her closer. "I haven't always recognized a good thing when I had it. I've made mistakes."

Pulse quickening, Bunny laughed shakily. "Tell me about it. Fortunately, for most, our mistakes make us who we are."

"But I'm not here to talk about the past." He gathered her into his arms, smoothing a strand of hair off her cheek and tucking it behind her ear. "I finally know what I want."

Bunny stared up into Jack's smoky brown eyes, her breath caught in her lungs. "You do?"

"I do." His lips touched hers, warm, sensuous and inviting.

"But I barely know you," Bunny whispered against his mouth.

"We've seen each other every week for the past six months." He skimmed her lips with his tongue, pressing through her teeth.

Bunny closed her eyes, her body melting against his, her resistance weakening. When he allowed her up for air, she asked, "Why now?"

He nipped at her earlobe and left a trail of kisses along her throat. "I'm ready."

"What if I'm not?" Bunny let her head drop back, her skin on fire, every nerve in her system antici-pating his touch. Who was she kidding? This cop had been one of her fantasies since the first time he'd stepped through the door of her flower shop.

He tipped her chin up and gazed into her eyes. "Then I have to convince you."

Her hands circled the back of his neck, and she pulled his head down until his lips crushed hers.

Jack shoved aside the food and wine glasses and laid her down on the tablecloth, his mouth never leaving hers. When he finally came up for air, he smiled down at her. "Is this helping to convince you?"

"Starting to." Everything that had happened to her so far that day led to her instant arousal and desire to see this through. But all the starts and stops were beginning to frustrate her, and her core ached for fulfillment only his hard cock could give her. She had forgotten she was in her shop, forgotten they were on the floor of her workroom. Forgotten the lunch he'd gone to so much trouble to acquire. All she could see was Jack. All she could feel was his body pressed to hers, his mouth sliding down over her sundress, kissing her breasts through the fabric. His hand slipped beneath her dress, feathering through her pubic hairs to find her clit.

Bunny arched her back off the floor, her knees splaying wide, giving him all the access he needed to seal this deal.

She wanted to feel his skin against hers, to have his hands caressing her body, tweaking, plucking and tempting her into complete surrender.

The shop bell jangled, shattering her concentration, jerking her back to the reality of where she was and what she was doing. Bunny sat up, yanking her dress over her hips. "I'll be right with you," she called out.

Jack pushed to his feet and grabbed her hand, pulling her up beside him, his brows furrowed. "This isn't over, you know."

She stared up into his face. "It has to be…for now."

He pressed a kiss to her lips, his hands threading through her hair. "I have a lot more convincing to do before we're done."

"It'll have to be when the shop is closed. This is insane."

"Bunny?" A gratingly familiar voice called out.

Shit. Ray. What the hell was he doing back?

Bunny stepped through the door into the front of the shop. "What do you want, Ray?"

Her ex-husband stared at her, his brows furrowing, his lips pressed into a tight line. Then his gaze shifted to the man who moved up behind her. "What's he still doing here?"

"He's…helping me." Bunny stumbled over her response. "Not that it's any business of yours."

Jack leaned close to her. "I need to run. Are you going to be all right? Do you want me to get rid of him before I leave?" The cop glared at Ray.

Bunny had to choke back her laughter at the way Ray's eyes widened. "No, I can handle him. You need to get to work."

Still, Jack hesitated a moment longer, then nodded toward the back room. "I'll collect the basket later." When he turned to go, Bunny laid a hand on his arm.

"Jack?"

"Yes, darlin'?" His hand went to her hip automatically.

The gesture warmed her heart as well has her hip. "Thanks…for lunch." Bunny leaned up on her tiptoes, grasped the back of his head and pulled him down for a deep, satisfying kiss.

Jack chuckled. "Maybe next time we'll actually eat."

The sound of Ray clearing his throat made her pull away, slowly. Reluctantly. "I'll see you tomorrow."

Jack's hand slipped down to squeeze her ass. "Count on it."

She slapped at him playfully and smiled as he left through the front door. Then her focus shifted to Ray, her happiness leaving with Jack.

Ray's lip curled into a snarl. "Do you realize how slutty you look?"

Bunny's hand lifted automatically to smooth her hair. "You can leave now."

"You should be ashamed of the way you're acting with the college boy and that cop."

While rage ripped through her, she forced a slow, sexy smile. "Jealous?"

"Not in the least. I'm about to be a married man."

"You were a married man once before. Adultery didn't seem to bother you. I'm not married now. Why should a single woman having fun with a couple of single guys be wrong?" She lifted a stack of gift cards from the counter and straightened them before laying them back down. "Is there some business that you forgot to attend to from this morning? Otherwise, this conversation is over."

"This conversation is over when I say it's over." Ray stepped closer to the counter. "I still own half of this business and I can call in the note anytime I feel like it."

Gooseflesh rose on Bunny's arm. "Are you threatening me?"

"I still have a stake in this business. If it fails, you won't be able to pay me back my eight thousand dollars."

"I'll pay back your lousy eight grand if I have to

haul trash to do it. Not that you did anything to deserve it."

Ray snorted. "According to the court system, I'm entitled."

Heat suffused her face. "Get out."

"I will, when I'm damned well ready."

Holding back every curse word she had ever imagined calling the bastard, Bunny pointed to the door. "Now."

"I'm leaving. But only because I have an appointment with the tuxedo rental place, not because you're telling me to." He stared down his nose at her, the sneer firmly in place. "I'm watching you, so get your act straight, or I'll shut you down faster than you can say whore."

Bunny shoved her fists into her pockets to keep from slapping the asshole.

When he left, she leaned against a wall and willed the negative energy out of her body. Two years ago, she'd promised herself to never let him get to her again. She'd broken that promise today. Thank goodness he wouldn't be at the Garden Club party that night, or she'd be tempted to tell him where he could put his eight thousand dollars.

CHAPTER FIVE

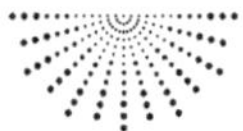

Cory stood in the elaborate garden of Mrs. Henry Sandell's, the president of the Temptation Garden Club. She'd chosen the timing of the party well. Every rose was blooming to perfection, and the lantana added bright spots of yellow-orange along the flagstone pathway, circling the acre of expertly planned and maintained flora.

Barely taking in the beauty of the surroundings, Cory kept his gaze glued to the gated entrance through which the members of the club entered and exited. He glanced at his watch. Half past the scheduled hour, and Bunny had yet to show.

"Cory, honey, can I tempt you with some punch?" Audrey, with Jackson at her side, stopped beside him and held out a dainty crystal punch cup.

He eyed the tiny cup and shook his head. "Rather have a beer."

Jackson chuckled. "You and me both, buddy." The

Kiowa Indian tugged at his stiff collar and shrugged his shoulders in the sports jacket, apparently as uncomfortable in the setting as Cory.

"She hasn't arrived yet, has she?" Audrey asked, her gaze shifting to the gate.

"No." For the hundredth time, Cory glanced at his watch. "How does this work? Are people supposed to be here at a certain time for a meeting or something?"

"Not tonight," Audrey said. "This is Mrs. Sandell's night to show off what she's done with her garden and answer any questions someone might ask, like the names of the flowers, the soil composition, watering, that kind of thing. It's casual. No formal structure."

Thank God. Bunny and Lacey would take a quick spin around the garden and they could leave. He could take Bunny home and start his courtship.

Movement by the garden gate jerked Cory's attention back to the people entering. He perked up and waited. When Ray Sinke and his fiancée, Chrissy, stepped through, Cory's shoulders sagged.

Great.

That would really put Bunny in the mood to be wooed. With an ex like Ray around, what chances did Cory or Jack stand? The bastard was a reminder that men were jerks and why Bunny should never get involved with them, ever again.

Cory's shoulders straightened. Well, he'd just have to show her otherwise by setting a better example and giving her what she needed. Tender, loving care...and an incredible orgasm. He was grinning by the time Lacey Lambert walked through the gate, followed by

Bunny, wearing the simple sundress and sandals she'd had on earlier that day.

From where he stood, he couldn't tell if she had a panty line, or if she was still naked beneath the dress. His cock stiffened. To hide the evidence, he crossed his hands at the wrist, dangling his cowboy hat over his crotch.

He got an erection every time he thought of the morning in the flower shop. The memory of Bunny's female musk still played havoc with his senses, even though it had been hours since he'd been with her.

She was laughing at something Lacey said when she glanced up and met his gaze. Her laughter ceased, and her eyes widened.

Cory waited, hoping it was a happy surprise for her to see him.

When a smile spread across Bunny's face, Cory let go of the breath he'd been holding and hurried forward.

"Lacey, so good to see you." He bent to plant a kiss on Lacey's cheek. "How's that brother of mine? You keeping him busy with the ranch?"

She patted his cheek and waggled her brow. "The poor man barely has time to water the horses, he's kept so busy with…projects…in the house." She leaned close to his ear. "More specifically, projects in the bedroom." Lacey winked and grabbed Bunny's arm. "I understand Bunny owns you and Jack."

"For one date," Bunny added quickly.

"Just one?" Lacey pouted. "You're in for a real treat. Cory is quite the lover."

Bunny's brows rose, her gaze shifting to Cory as color rose in her cheeks. "Is that so?"

Lacey patted her arm. "He helped me and Nick get together in a little harmless ménage, didn't you, sweetie?" She patted his cheek again. "Now I can't imagine what I'd do with another man. Nick's more than enough to keep me happy."

Cory cringed at Lacey's casual remark about the ménage. "That was before I met Bunny. I haven't looked twice or touched another woman since. Where's Nick?"

Lacey sighed. "He's on a business trip to New York. Something about an investment he wants to make."

"Ah yes, he told me about that. I hope he manages to clinch the deal. I'm in it for half." Cory dared to look toward Bunny, wondering how she was taking Lacey's little revelation. "Are you mad?'

Bunny's brows scrunched, her color high in both cheeks. "About what?"

"That Lacey and I had a one-night stand with my brother?"

Bunny's shoulder rose. "I really don't own you, and like I told Jack, our past is what makes us who we are today." Her lips tipped upward and she leaned close. "Truth is, I think it's kind of sexy."

Cory rubbed his chin, a small smile tugging at the corners of his mouth. "I know I learned a few things from that incident with Lacey and Nick. It was quite the educational opportunity." He held out his arm. "Care to stroll through Mrs. Sandell's garden?"

Lacey patted Bunny's back. "You two go on. I want to talk to Audrey and Jackson. And if you decide to leave early, that's fine. I can hang with them."

With the path clear for an early departure, Cory could hardly wait to get Bunny out of there. He had to pace himself to keep from jogging Bunny through the acre of garden.

After walking halfway around the garden path, Bunny paused in front of a bush full of blood-red roses. "These are lovely."

Cory stared down at Bunny. Her dark brown hair caught the dying light from the setting sun, which brought out the red highlights and gave her a golden halo. His heart swelling against his ribs, Cory's arm tightened against his side, trapping her hand. "Beautiful."

Bunny glanced up and caught him staring. "You aren't even looking at the roses."

"No, because nothing, not even a garden full of roses holds a candle to you."

Her cheeks pinkened, and her head ducked low. "That kind of flattery can go to a girl's head."

"It's only true." He nudged her chin with his finger, tipping it upward.

"I didn't know you would be here tonight." She leaned against his arm and walked on. "Did Lacey?"

Cory's cheeks heated. "I hadn't planned on coming until you told me you'd be here. Suffice it to say I had to beg my sweet almost-sister-in-law to secure an invite for me or I wouldn't be here at all."

Bunny's eyes narrowed. "Why exactly *are* you here?"

"Because you are. I wanted to spend more time with you."

Her frown deepened. "That's what Jack said."

Cory's eyes narrowed. "Did you see him again today?" He held his breath, half-wishing Jack hadn't had time to meet with Bunny at lunch.

She nodded with a tender smile on her face. "He was so sweet, helping me deliver flowers. I don't know what I would have done without his assistance. Then we had…lunch in the shop." She glanced away, her cheeks turning a deeper pink.

Had Jack scored? It was on the tip of Cory's tongue to ask, but he bit down hard to keep from letting the words pop out. To be fair to his friend, he couldn't begrudge him the equal opportunity to win the flower girl's heart. He sighed. "To tell you the truth, we both have it bad for you."

Bunny's eyes widened. "Why?"

Cory chuckled. "Why? Because you're you."

"Don't be silly. I'm just the owner of a small flower shop."

"You're so much more than that to us."

"That's silly." She shook her head and looked away, twin flags of color riding high on her cheekbones.

Cory cupped her face in his palms and turned her to face him. "I love the way you greet everyone with a smile. You always say something nice to your customers. You go out of your way to make them happy. I know that you donated all the decorations for the Cowboy Auction..." He dragged in a deep breath and finished with, "...and you're the most beautiful woman I've ever met."

"Cory, you're younger than me. You have all the firsts to experience. Your first love, your first marriage. I'm damaged goods. I've already been around the block with a first marriage. I don't understand why you'd want to be with me."

"I told you before, I might be younger, but I've seen a lot. As a stripper at the Ugly Stick, I've seen it all, good and bad. I like that you're not flighty, that you know what you want and can make your own decisions." He smiled. "I like that when you smile, you get little wrinkles around your eyes." Cory smoothed a thumb across the corners of her eyes.

BUNNY LIFTED a hand to cover the crow's feet, suddenly self-conscious of the evidence of her aging. "Thanks for reminding me." The fine wrinkles had made their appearance last year no matter how much moisturizer she rubbed into them.

He pulled her fingers away. "They're beautiful—a part of you. Don't hide them." Cory bent to kiss the corner of her eye.

"You can be very convincing." Her eyelids fluttering closed, Bunny leaned into the hard muscles of Cory's chest. She no longer stood in Mrs. Sandell's garden. She was alone with Cory, far away from the snoopy, tongue-waggers. And she wasn't wearing panties. Her pussy clenched, and she snuggled closer, her hands circling Cory's waist.

His kiss feathered down her cheek to claim her lips in a soul-scorching caress.

Never in her life had Bunny been as turned on by just a kiss. Her body burst into flame, her insides aching so badly she could barely breathe. The day's temptations had stockpiled into an explosive combination of need and lust.

"Damn, Bunny. You'd think one man was enough. Everywhere I turn, you're hanging all over another. And here in public?" Ray's raised voice jerked Bunny out of the cocoon of longing.

Bunny would have jumped back, but Cory's arm held her against him. He smiled down at her, the simple gesture reassuring, calming the heat in Bunny's cheeks.

Chrissy laid a hand on her fiancé's arm. "Ray, please, don't make a scene."

"Scene?" Ray snorted. "I'm not the one making a scene. These two might as well be filming a porn movie. And here in Mrs. Sandell's backyard."

"Please," Chrissy begged.

"What seems to be the problem?" Mrs. Sandell, trailed by Mrs. Biedel and Mrs. Rutherford, the three head matriarchs of the Temptation Garden Club, converged on them.

Audrey, Lacey and Jackson hurried forward from across the yard.

"I'll tell you what the problem is," Ray said, waving

a hand at Bunny and Cory. "These two are practically fornicating in front of everyone."

Cory stiffened. "Apologize, Mr. Sinke."

"Or what? You'll prove me right and do it with my wife, here on the grass?"

Chrissy gasped, her face turning bright red.

Rage burned through Bunny, her heartbeat pounding through heated veins.

"She's not your wife. You gave up that privilege two years ago." Cory raised his clenched fist. "Now apologize to her."

Afraid he'd throw a punch, Bunny laid a hand on his arm. "Don't. He's not worth it."

"What's the matter, Bunny? Can't get a real man, so you'll settle for this little boy who gets naked for money, like the whore he is?"

That was it. The final straw in a long line of slights her ex had heaped on her over the years. Before she could stop herself, she balled her fist and slammed it into Ray's smirking face.

Ray staggered back, knocking into Chrissy and sending her flying into a blood-red rose bush.

Pain shot through Bunny's knuckles, but she refused to show it. "That's for being rude to my friend. And he's more of a man than you ever were or ever will be."

Jackson fished Chrissy out of the rose bush and set her on her feet. Tears streamed down her cheeks. "Ray, look what you did." She stared at the pricks of blood on her arms where the thorns had torn her skin. Then she glared at Ray through blue eyes awash in tears. "And I was going to look so beautiful in my wedding dress Saturday." She covered her face and ran from the garden, sobbing.

Guilt hit Bunny like a Mack truck. No matter how she felt about Ray, Chrissy deserved better. She was just a young, naive girl suckered into Ray's world. Bunny touched Cory's arm. "I'm sorry. I shouldn't have done that."

"You're damn right you shouldn't have." Ray rose from the ground, his face blotchy red, his lip split and bleeding. "You'll be hearing from my lawyer."

Her heart sank to the lowest point in her belly. "Okay, then." She glanced at Cory with a twisted smile. "I have to leave. Tell Jack the date's off." Then she hurried to find Lacey, leaving Cory standing in the middle of the crowd.

So much for finding love in a garden. Now Ray was riled. He'd go for the throat and put her out of business. Damn. Tomorrow, she'd have to eat crow and apologize to Ray and figure her way out of this mess.

CORY STARTED to follow Bunny out of the garden, but Audrey caught his arm. "Let her go."

"This is all my fault." He shook off her hand and would have sprinted after Bunny but Jackson stepped in front of him.

"Sometimes you have to back up and really look at what's driving a woman to understand how you can help and earn her love and respect."

"Tell him, Jackson." Audrey winked at her man. "What does Bunny value most?"

Cory tore his gaze off the garden gate where Bunny had disappeared and tried to focus on what Jackson and Audrey were telling him. After a moment he shook his head. "Her shop?"

Audrey nodded. "Her shop signifies her independence. It was the only thing in her life she had any kind of control over. If she loses her shop, she loses her means to support herself. She'll be flat on her ass and dependent on others to make a living."

"I can afford to support her."

Jackson shook his head. "And I could afford to support Audrey, but she wouldn't let me."

"Right. I went into this relationship on equal footing with Jackson," Audrey said. "I'm here because I *want* to be, not because I *have* to be. Been in that situation and never want to go back. I'm a business-woman. I need a business to run."

"Bunny has been supporting herself and her jerk ex-husband for so long, if you pull the shop out from under her, she'll be devastated."

"But you heard Ray. He's going after her."

"And he holds half of the deck in his hands."

Cory frowned. "What do you mean?"

"The judge awarded him half of all of Bunny's assets in the divorce."

"So he owns half of her shop?" Cory shook his head. "That's insane."

"Texas is a common law state. Everything was split in the divorce."

"Damn." Cory shoved a hand through his hair. "What can I do to keep him from closing her down?"

"You and Jack are pretty good with investments." Audrey smiled. "Put your financial acumen to work and figure it out. But don't make it seem like the two of you want to take care of everything for her. If you're serious about wooing Bunny, you'll have to give her the opportunity to go into it on equal footing."

Jackson kissed Audrey. "I couldn't have put it better. Cory's got a lot to think about, so we should leave him to it. Ready to go?"

She laughed and kissed him back. "Yup." She touched Cory's shoulder. "Bunny's a good person. Just don't break her heart."

Cory stood for a long moment in the garden, his mind cranking through all that had happened. When he came up with a solution, he pulled out his cell phone and dialed Jack. "You at the house?"

"I am," Jack responded. "How'd it go with Bunny?"

"Put on the coffee. We have some thinkin' to do."

"That bad, huh?"

"Let's just say the courtin' isn't going quite as planned."

Jack snorted. "Tell me about it."

Cory hit End.

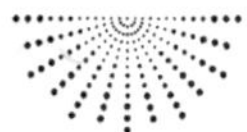

CHAPTER SIX

Jack and Cory had called several times that day, each asking her to reconsider and go through with the date.

She'd turned them down every time, until she'd finished all the flower arrangements for Ray and Chrissy's wedding. Her rebellious streak had kicked in around five o'clock. After stewing all day about Ray and his lawyer, she'd worried herself into a frazzle.

The phone rang exactly at five. At that point, she'd had enough. Enough of Ray being an ass. Enough worrying about how she'd pay the flower wholesaler if Ray called in his note. And enough celibacy to last a lifetime. If she was going to lose her business, by golly, she'd go down with one last really good orgasm.

"Bunny, it's Jack. Would you please reconsid—"

"I'll go," she blurted.

"You will?" Jack chuckled. "What changed your mind?"

"Let's just say, I'm tired of being at the mercy of everyone else. I'll be ready at six." She hung up before she could change her mind.

Her heart racing, she'd rushed up the stairs to her apartment, changed into a daisy-print cotton sundress and white sandals. At the last minute, she yanked her panties off and tossed them. They landed on a lampshade, and she didn't even try to retrieve them.

Now, as she sat in Mona's beauty shop, warm air wafted up her dress, reminding her of the two men who'd soon be by to pick her up.

"I think you should wear it up, with a few tendrils emphasizing your long, gorgeous neck." Mona had insisted on Bunny coming to her salon at five fifteen for a quick shampoo and style.

"I still can't believe I'm going through with this date. I have enough trouble without adding fuel to the fire."

"You can't let what Ray said have you runnin' scared." Mona wrapped another strand of hair around the iron and held it. "Did you stop in at the bank?"

"I filled out a loan application as soon as it opened. The loan officer said he'd get back to me after he ran it by their underwriter."

"There you go. Problem solved."

Bunny wished it was that easy. She was already in hock for half the loan on the business, and making payments was giving her hell with cash flow. When Mona tried to pin the strand of hair up and away from her face, Bunny swatted her hand. "Leave it down. Up would be too formal for this dress." Bunny squirmed in the seat, fully aware of her nakedness beneath the dress. All day long, between work and worry, she'd teetered on the verge of another orgasm. The anticipation and the frustration had made her so tense, she could barely concentrate. She'd dropped two vases and cut her finger picking up shards of glass. Twice she'd almost called Jack and Cory and begged them to come scratch her itch to put her out of her misery. Too stubborn and scared to follow through, she trudged through the day until she finally buckled at Jack's last phone call.

"I'm glad you changed your mind and decided to go on this date." As Mona curled and smoothed Bunny's hair, she sighed. "I'm so green with envy, I can hardly see straight."

Her nerves on edge, Bunny grabbed Mona's hand. "Why don't you come with me?"

Mona shook her head. "Much as I'd love to, this is your date. I've never dated two men at once. I want to know what it's like. All the details." She whipped the cape from Bunny's shoulders and handed her the mirror. "What do you think?"

Bunny stared at her hair from all angles, a smile tugging at her lips. She'd never looked better. "Thanks for turning this sow's ear into a silk purse." Bunny pushed to her feet, her dress clinging high to her thighs. Before she could pull it down, Mona's eyes widened.

"Bunny Leigh." Mona's mouth curved into a smile. "Are you wearing underwear?"

Bunny tried to dart away.

Mona grabbed the hem of her dress before she could and flipped it up. "Oh, good Lord, the woman's going commando!"

Bunny's cheeks flamed. "Don't tell anyone, for heaven's sakes."

"Your secret is safe with me." Mona fanned herself. "I'm getting hot over the thought." Her eyes grew even wider. "And you sat in my chair the whole time, naked-assed. I'm gonna come." Her fingers slid down over her breasts. "Sweet Jesus, it's gonna be a long night with my vibrator." She glanced over Bunny's shoulder. "And here they come. Two of the hottest men in the state."

Bunny spun toward the big salon windows, her pulse hammering.

Cory drove up to the curb in a vintage model convertible with a wide bench seat. He shifted into park, and he and Jack climbed out. Both men wore crisp white shirts, starched blue jeans and dark cowboy hats.

"You don't think I'm a cradle robber, do you?" Bunny's knees shook and her courage waned as the two men stepped up on the sidewalk.

"Hell, no. Those two have their heads on straight and have earned the respect of the people of this town. And you look absolutely stunning." She shoved Bunny toward the door. "Get out there and get some for us single ladies. Man, I'd love to be in your panties." Mona grinned. "No, wait. You're not wearing any."

Mona's laughter followed Bunny as she stepped out of the salon, catching Cory as he tried the door to the flower shop next door. "Over here."

Jack reached her first, swept her into his arms and bent her over for a long, romantic kiss, his hand sliding down to cup her ass.

"Commando," Mona murmured from her door, sighing. "Go get 'em, tiger."

Cory took his turn, pressing her hips to his. His hard cock nudged her belly, making her pussy cream in anticipation of that big hard shaft driving into her again and again. "Feel that?"

Boy, did she. Heat rushed over every part of Bunny's body. "I thought you were taking me to dinner?"

Jack sandwiched her from behind. "I'd rather start with dessert."

"Much as I agree..." Cory stepped away. "We promised to take Bunny on a *real* date."

Bunny sucked in a deep breath, pushing aside the disappointment that they wouldn't be starting with dessert. "Where are we going?"

Jack grinned and Cory answered, "The county fair."

"The fair?" Bunny couldn't think of a less sexy place. And all she had on her mind was getting naked with these two and finishing what they'd started in the shop the day before. "Really?"

Cory laughed. "Don't look so disappointed. It's outside of Temptation, but only a few miles. The fair is pretty much neutral ground where we can build the anticipation for later."

"The dessert part." Jack pressed his hand to the small of her back. "Let's get going. The sooner we have fun at the fair, the sooner we get to have dessert."

With a glare at his partner, Cory climbed behind the wheel. "We're supposed to show her how to have fun."

"I'll show her fun," Jack promised.

Bunny laughed and slid between the two of them, shivering at the decadence of having two men accompany her. She cast a glance back at the salon where Mona waved from the window.

That would have been her before she'd taken the step to the wild side and bid on these two incorrigible men. She decided to enjoy it—her last hurrah—and, if for no other reason, to have tales to tell Mona later.

Ha!

She was looking forward to being with Cory and Jack for herself, not for Mona. A sad thought pushed its way into her subconscious. When the date was over, Cory and Jack would have no obligation to go out with her again. She'd be on her own to find her next date. Like Mona said, going out at all, even a bought-and-paid-for date, was just what she'd needed to get her out of her slump. Especially with Ray and Chrissy's wedding flowers to deliver tomorrow and her business to save next week.

Bunny had to admit, she'd dreaded Ray's wedding. After slugging him the night before, she was afraid he'd give her hell while she set up the floral arrangements. She'd almost backed out and told them to find another flower shop. Then pride kicked in, and she knew she had to go through with it. And maybe if Chrissy was pleased with the results, she'd have some sway over Ray and get him to back off closing her down.

Tomorrow was tomorrow. Bunny sat back, basking in the late afternoon sunshine, determined to live it up today. She was on her way to the fair with the best-looking dates a girl could ask for. And later? Well, who knew what they had planned? She had plans of her own.

Cory pulled onto Main Street and slid his hand onto her knee.

Jack handled the other leg, each man's fingers sliding upward and under her dress until they both threaded through the curly hairs at the apex of her thighs.

"Hot damn!" Jack whistled. "No panties. My sweet tooth is getting damned horny." Jack adjusted his jeans.

"Keep it in your pants, dude." Cory smiled. "Although, I can feel your pain." Cory pressed a finger between her folds and flicked her clit.

"Oh, sweet Jesus." Bunny almost came.

"Hey." Jack pointed to the road ahead. "Keep your eyes on the road and your hands on the wheel. I'd like to live to dessert."

Cory flicked Bunny again, then returned his hand to the steering wheel to make the turn onto the road leading to the fair grounds.

Jack slipped into place where Cory had left off, his fingers parting her folds to stroke her.

By the time they reached the fairgrounds, Bunny was in a freakin' lather and in no shape to stand and walk around with her pussy throbbing and her thighs shaking.

Thank goodness both men insisted on taking an arm and leading her through the parking lot to the entrance.

In an attempt to regain her equilibrium, Bunny asked, "How did you two become such close friends?"

"Who said we were friends?" Jack quipped.

Cory's lips twisted. "We met backstage at the Ugly Stick Saloon two years ago."

"Before I got on with the sheriff's department," Jack added. "I taught the young whelp everything I know about stripping."

"Get real. You taught me about fighting." Cory snorted. "Kendall taught me all she knew about dancing. You could stand to take a lesson or two from her."

"My strippin' days are over. The sheriff doesn't look kindly on strip- lightin'." Jack grinned down at her. "That's what I call moonlightin' as a stripper."

Bunny smiled up at him. The biggest difference between these men and Ray was that her dates understood what made a woman hot and horny, and they cared what she wanted. Oh yes, she was going to love dessert tonight. "How long are we staying at the fair?" she asked.

Cory laughed. "Ready to leave?"

Not wanting to appear too anxious to get to the

sex part of this date, Bunny forced a shrug. "Just wondering."

"We'll leave when we've visited all the booths and ridden all the rides."

Bunny swallowed hard on the moan rising up her throat.

"All the rides?" Jack groaned. "Really?" He leaned in front of Bunny and whispered loud enough for Cory to hear, and anyone else within five feet for that matter, "She's not wearing panties, man. Do you know what that's doing to me?"

A smile tugged at the corners of Bunny's lips. "Not nearly what it's doing to me," she muttered.

"I heard that." Cory grabbed her hand and headed for the merry-go-round. "Let's ride."

Bunny wanted to ride all right, but not a toy horse. She wanted to ride Cory and Jack.

After Cory bought tickets, they stood in line with a couple little kids and finally it was their turn to climb on board the merry-go-round.

Cory mounted a black horse close to the center, pulling Bunny up in his lap. He settled her sidesaddle, his hand slipping under her dress. "Told you we'd have fun."

Jack mounted the horse beside them, his gaze on Bunny's dress where Cory's hand disappeared beneath. "I see where this is going. I got the next ride."

As the music started and the ride spun slowly, the horse moved up and down on the pole. Bunny had a little problem forcing a smile for the mothers waiting on the outside of the fence.

Cory had her gasping within seconds, clinging to the pole as tingles built to shudders. With each rotation of the ride, Bunny found it harder and harder to smile and wave. By the time the ride came to a halt, she was clinging to the pole as though her life depended on it.

Jack dismounted first, grabbed her around the waist and helped her to her feet. "If you liked that, wait for the bumper cars."

"But first we need to shoot something." Cory got down a little slower, walking funny, as if his jeans were too tight in all the wrong places.

Bunny suppressed a smile of triumph. At least she hadn't been the only one affected by the ride.

With her pussy throbbing, she was forced to play spectator at a BB gun booth, while Jack and Cory demonstrated their prowess at shooting. When they failed to win her the huge pink teddy bear, she touched both of their shoulders, frustrated and ready to move on. "Let me try."

Taking careful aim, she focused on all her father had taught her back when he'd been alive, and she fired bull's-eyes, one after the other. They walked away arguing over who had to carry the giant pink bear.

A dinner of hot dogs smothered in relish and mustard was followed by the promised bumper cars. Cory teamed with the pink teddy bear, while Jack joined Bunny in the car and insisted on her driving.

Bunny couldn't imagine how Jack would top Cory's merry-go-round near-orgasm. As soon as the ride commenced, Bunny had her hands full of steering wheel, and Jack had his hand full of her pussy.

Every time Bunny slammed into the back of another car, Jack's finger thrust deep into her.

The more he thrust, the more she searched for another car to hit until the carny blew a whistle and made them leave for being too aggressive.

Shamefaced and frustrated by the sexual foreplay and teasing, Bunny had just about reached her limit. "Can we go now?"

Cory shook his head and pointed up.

Bunny stared at the giant Ferris wheel and moaned. This would be yet another teasing ride that would leave her wanting more and still lacking the ultimate fulfillment her body craved. She was beginning to wonder if it would be another night of dissatisfaction with her vibrator. At least all three of them, and the teddy bear, would have plenty of room to sit in the same large, bucket seat.

To hell with that. As the operator waved them onto the ride, Bunny slapped a fifty-dollar bill in his hand and whispered into his ear. The greasy man grinned and nodded.

Cory sat in the seat and pulled her over close to him. "What were you talking to the operator about?"

"Just asking if the ride has experienced any malfunctions lately," Bunny replied, fighting but not quite winning against the smile that slipped across her lips.

"And?" Jack adjusted the big pink teddy bear in the seat beside him, forcing him to edge closer to Bunny.

"It's been known to have a few hiccups," she replied, ducking her head to keep her smile from giving her away.

"Maybe we shouldn't ride it." Cory started to rise.

Bunny pressed his thigh until he sat. "He assured me it was perfectly safe."

"I don't trust it." Jack leaned forward to stand.

With a hand on his thigh, close enough to brush his straining cock, Bunny urged him to remain seated. "It'll be fine. I promise."

Both Cory and Jack frowned. The ride jerked ominously as their chair started its rise to the top.

Bunny counted the empty chairs between them and the next one with people in it. So far only three couples had boarded the ride. All seemed intent on smooching along the way. Bunny had plans of her own. She was determined to make this their last ride, so they could move on to somewhere more intimate and private.

When they'd reached a quarter turn, she raised her hands from their thighs to skim across to the bulges beneath their jeans. Jack was more than ready and Cory, despite his insistence on going on a *real* date, was hard and stiff beneath the denim.

"Watch it, lady. That's a loaded weapon you're touching," Jack said in his best John Wayne impression.

"I'm counting on it." Bunny loosened Cory's belt.

Cory caught her hand as she flicked his button free. "I hope you know what you're doing."

"I'm taking advice from a wise young man." She freed Jack's belt buckle and top button. Then with her hand on both of their zippers at once, she eased them down, surprised and delighted that they too were going commando. Her channel slicked in anticipation, and she prayed the fifty was enough to get the operator to do what should come in about three…two…one…seconds. The Ferris wheel jerked to a stop with their car at the very top.

Bunny smiled. "Now it's my turn to get a couple of guys as hot as this girl is." She freed both of their cocks and circled them with her palms.

Cory chuckled.

Jack gasped. "This will be a first for me. I've never done more than kiss at the top of the Ferris wheel."

"And you?" Bunny asked Cory.

"I've done a little more than kiss." Cory threaded a hand through her hair and smiled. "The woman who was afraid of going out with two guys has a naughty side after all."

"I blame it on you two." Bunny's hand tightened around Cory's cock. "Just say the word…" She leaned down until her lips touched the tip of his dick. "And I'll stop." Her tongued curled around his head, lapping at the firm, silky skin, stretched taught over his thickness. He had at least two inches on Ray and was twice as thick.

Bunny's pussy clenched. She wanted to feel that shaft inside her. She did the next best thing and pressed down over him, sliding his cock deep into her mouth.

Behind her, Jack lifted her dress and slid his finger into her warm, wet cunt, pumping to the rhythm of her movements over Cory's cock. "That's right, Bunny, let's get this party started."

Over and over, she came down on Cory, until his fingers laced through her hair and he pulled her off. "Stop, before I come," he said through gritted teeth.

Bunny smiled and licked her lips before turning to Jack. "Ready?"

"You have no idea." He cupped the back of her neck and pulled her close to kiss her, then guided her head down to his lap and thrust his cock into her mouth.

Bunny took all of him until he bumped the back of her throat. She'd given Ray a blowjob on occasion, but he'd never returned the favor. Bunny felt a certain sense of power over these men and sucked hard on Jack's cock, knowing in her gut, dessert was going to be the best part of this night.

Cory nudged her ass with his finger, finding the tight little hole of her anus, and pressed against it.

Bunny gasped around Jack's dick and sucked it deeper.

Jack's hands dug into her hair and urged her to go faster.

Cory slipped two fingers into Bunny's cunt as the Ferris wheel lurched forward.

"No," Jack moaned. "Not yet."

One more time, Bunny sucked his cock, then

pulled off, sitting up straight and dragging her dress back down over her bottom.

The men struggled to zip, button and buckle their belts before the ride came to a halt and they had to get off.

Bunny patted her hair in place and stepped off, flipping her skirt up just enough to show Jack and Cory a little ass. If they chose to ignore that invitation, so be it. She'd ask to be dropped off at her apartment so that she could finish what they'd started on her own.

"What next?" she asked, her face schooled into an innocent smile.

Cory growled, grabbed her hand and marched her toward the exit.

Jack hooked her other elbow, his face determined and tense. "Time for goddamn dessert."

CHAPTER SEVEN

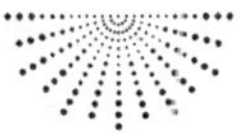

Bunny sat quietly between the two men as they pulled out of the fairground's parking lot and onto the highway headed back to Temptation. The pink teddy bear was relegated to the back seat, strapped into a seat belt to keep it from flying out. Neither man had spoken since the Ferris wheel ride.

Both of them sat tense, hands to themselves.

Bunny worried her bottom lip, wondering if she'd gone too far and scared them off. Did men like women who took control? Ray never had. It put a kink in his ego every time. Everything Bunny had done to keep food on the table and pay the rent had to appear to be a team effort when, in fact, it had all been her effort.

As they neared town, she sank lower into her seat, fearing the worst. Jack and Cory would drop her off at her apartment and leave her high and dry. She'd be humiliated and forced to get off on her vibrator—a cold substitute for what these guys could provide in the way of thrust and vibration.

When they passed the turn to her apartment, Bunny sat up, hope blooming. "Where are we going?"

"To our place," Cory said.

This being his first communication since they'd left the fair, Bunny was still very turned on, but didn't want to appear too eager. "What if I don't want to go?"

Cory slammed his foot on the brake and Bunny pitched forward, saved by her seat belt.

"After the Ferris wheel?" He stared at her, brows raised. "You're telling me you don't want to go home with us?"

Heat filled Bunny's cheeks. "No, that's not what I'm telling you. But a girl likes to be asked." Hell, yeah, she wanted to go to their place. "And if we're going to your place, you missed your turn."

Cory shifted his foot from the brake to the accelerator. "I moved."

"Really?" She hadn't known that. For as long as she remembered, Cory had lived around the corner from her flower shop. He drove his convertible or rode his bike past her windows practically every day. It was one of the highlights of her morning.

"You're gonna love it." Jack grinned beside her. "We're doing the work ourselves."

Bunny shook her head. "I didn't know you two knew anything about carpentry."

"My dad is a building contractor in Austin," Jack

said. "I've been building houses since I was big enough to hold a hammer."

"I learn quickly," Cory added.

Bunny's estimation of Cory and Jack rose several notches. How much more did she not know about these men? "So why did you go into stripping?"

"I got that one." Jack laughed. "The money is so much better than working as a trim carpenter, and Cory could work nights while going to school during the day."

Bunny nodded. "Smart."

"There's more to this great body than meets the eye." Cory winked at her.

"I'm beginning to see that." Afraid to let the conversation peter off and leave her anxious and self-conscious about what was going to happen at Cory's new house, Bunny turned to Jack. "What's your story?"

"Started college…" Jack glanced away. "Was in a wreck and dropped out."

Bunny rested her hand on his arm. "Were you injured?"

He stared into the distance. "Some."

"Some, hell," Cory added. "Tell her." When Jack didn't fill in the blanks, Cory continued, "Jack was in a coma for a week. His girlfriend died in that wreck."

"Oh, Jack!" Bunny's hand slipped down to his. "That must have a huge shock."

He squeezed hers. "It was. She was gone and buried before I woke up. But that's the past."

"That's not something you forget, or want to

forget." Bunny stared at the hand she held. "What was her name?"

His grip had tightened almost painfully. "Stacy."

Bunny swallowed hard, the urgency to get naked with these men having calmed. She really didn't know them at all. "Is that why you quit school?"

He shrugged. "For a while, nothing seemed important."

"Makes me think my problems aren't so bad," Bunny whispered. "I'm sorry you lost her. You must have loved her very much."

He nodded. "Stacy loved life. Had I died, she'd have gone on living."

"Based on what you've told me about her," Cory added, "she would have wanted the same for you."

"How long ago was it?" Bunny asked.

Jack straightened. "Three years."

"He'd probably still be stripping at the Ugly Stick if—"

"Cory hadn't come along and talked me into going back to school." Jack chuckled. "He's a force to be reckoned with when he sets his mind on something."

Bunny bent her arm, bringing Jack's hand up to her cheek and leaned against his knuckles. "How did you get into stripping?"

"After Stacy passed, I went on a self-destructive binge. One night at the Ugly Stick, back before Audrey owned it, I got jumped by a couple of bikers. I'd been in fights before, but I didn't know how to defend myself against more than two at once."

Bunny gasped. "More than two?"

He nodded, his lips twisting into a grimace. "I was about Cory's age—young. Thought I knew everything and was invincible." Jack shrugged. "I learned that night that I wasn't, and I wanted to do something about it, and about guys like the bikers who beat me up."

Bunny frowned. "How does that play into stripping? You were stripping before Cory, right?"

Jack nodded. "Yeah, I got into it before Cory. Audrey was working there back then. She helped pick up the pieces and talked me into strippin'. It paid my way through self-defense training and the rest of my bachelor degree in Criminal Justice, once Cory convinced me to finish. Then I got on with the local sheriff's department."

"You made a heck of a comeback." Bunny leaned back in her seat.

"Jack taught me a lot about self-defense." Cory's lips pressed into a thin line. "I reckon I'd have been beat up a lot more times by jealous boyfriends otherwise."

Jack nodded. "One of the dangers of the stripper gig."

"I never thought of that." Bunny's eyes widened as they turned off the road and stopped at an arched gateway with a wooden sign sporting the words Rafter M Ranch across the top. "M as in Monahan?"

Cory nodded. "And McBride. Jack, my brother and I went together on the property. Nick finished his house a couple months back, and Jack and I are almost done with ours." The road split into a Y and Cory took the left fork.

"Why are you and Jack building a house together?"

"Since I'll be going to school in Dallas for the next few years, we decided to build one house between us. We get along better than brothers and didn't see a need to build another. If, down the road, we outgrow it, we have enough land to build another. For now, we're happy with the way things are."

Bunny couldn't see much past the headlights as they traveled up and down low-rising hills. On the final rise, the headlights shone on a structure perched at the top of the hill. As they moved closer Bunny's heartbeat stuttered. "A log cabin?"

Cory shrugged. "I always dreamed of living in the mountains, but when it came right down to it, I couldn't leave my home state of Texas. Jack and I brought a little mountain livin' home."

The steep roof rose into the night sky and giant windows stretched from floor to roof. A soft light glowed from a lamp in what looked like a massive living room.

"You did all this with the money you made stripping?" Bunny asked, her eyes rounded, her jaw hanging slack. "I'm in the wrong business."

"Told you she'd like it," Jack said. "Cory and I don't just strip. Tell her."

"We invested in the right stock." Cory stared up at the house. "It paid off."

"I'd say it did." Bunny turned to him. "And you're only twenty-one?"

"I'll be twenty-two in a month, if that helps." He grinned, shifted into park and climbed out of the convertible. "Wanna see the bedroom?" He extended his hand, a wicked smile stretching across his lips.

Still somewhat subdued by Jack's sad story, Bunny nodded, her pulse picking up in anticipation. She wanted to see the whole house more than the bedroom. The night was turning out to be a very enlightening experience. Not only about Cory and Jack. Bunny was learning to take the bull by the horns and demand what she wanted as well, instead of taking whatever leftovers remained. Her newfound confidence made her slide across the seat and take Cory's hand.

"That's my girl." He yanked her into his arms and planted a kiss on her lips. "I've wanted to do that since we left the fair."

She laughed huskily. "I've wanted to do a whole lot more than that since we were on the Ferris wheel."

"I believe our Bunny is turning into a bold woman." Jack joined them, clasping her hand.

"What happened to the fear of being considered a cougar?" Cory smiled down at her.

Bunny shrugged. "I'm getting over it...fast." She slipped her arms around the two men. "A week ago, I would never have pictured myself with two men."

Jack chuckled. "And look at you now."

"I didn't realize just how deep a rut I'd fallen into, until I bought you two."

Cory leaned close to her ear and whispered, "We'll never let you go back."

His warm breath and the soft words sent shivers across Bunny's skin. She didn't expect anything past tonight. After all, this was a paid-for date. These men had no obligation to call her the next day or week or ever again. But Cory's words gave her a sense of hope that she quickly pushed to the back of her mind.

This was a night she wanted to fill with memories of what it was like to be loved by two men. Not that love was involved. Lust, yes. But she could imagine.

As they climbed the steps arm-in-arm, Bunny's breathing became more labored, her heart racing against her ribs. She hadn't been completely naked with a man since her divorce. What if they didn't find her attractive?

She stopped in front of the door and stepped out of their arms. "This is pretty overwhelming. What if you two are disappointed?"

"What are you talking about?" Cory captured her hand. "You're a beautiful woman. How could we possibly be disappointed?"

Jack took her other hand. "Cory's right. You're gorgeous, intelligent, spunky, and your ex was a fool to let you go."

"But you haven't seen me naked." Bunny's head dipped, her cheeks burning. "What if we get inside, get naked and you don't like what you see?"

"We can solve that right here, right now…before we go in." Cory grinned, grabbed the hem of her dress and dragged it up her thighs and over her hips.

Bunny's hands pressed downward. "Out here? In the open?"

Jack smiled, his gaze on the track of the rising hem. "There's no one for miles. Just the three of us."

Bunny relaxed her arms and let Cory pull the dress up higher. The warm night breeze caressed her legs, stirring the hairs covering her mons, and brushed across her belly. She'd set off that evening on a journey to a powerful orgasm. Possibly her only opportunity to be with two men at once and experience the most exquisite orgasm ever. What did she have to lose? She raised her arms and the dress flew the rest of the way over her head.

Cory and Jack whistled as one.

Standing in nothing but her sandals, Bunny's body burned. But not with embarrassment.

Cory tipped his head and walked around her. "Nice, trim waist."

Jack took the cue from Cory and followed suit. "Sexy hips."

Cory lifted a strand of her hair as he walked behind her. "Great hair, long and thick, the kind a guy likes to run his hands through."

Jack slapped her bottom, making her jump. "Tight ass."

When Cory rounded to the front, his gaze centered on her breasts and he reached out and cupped one in his palm. "Perfect breasts."

Bunny tingled at his touch, ready to skip the foreplay and get right to hard and heavy sex.

Jack weighed the other breast in his hand. "About the size of a grapefruit, if I recall." He bent to take it in his mouth. "Yup. And much tastier."

Bunny moaned when he sucked on the nipple.

Then the two men stood back, leaving her alone, bared to their gazes and quickly becoming self-conscious at her nakedness when they were still fully clothed.

Cory glanced at Jack. "Well?"

Jack nodded. "She'll do."

Bunny laughed shakily and slapped Jack's arm. "Are you two going to make me stand here naked or invite me in?"

Cory crossed his arms. "Are you comfortable with the idea we find you absolutely, one hundred percent beautiful?"

She fought the urge to cover herself. This was her night, her fantasy. Why the hell should she be afraid? Bunny pushed her shoulders back, her breasts jutting forward, and tipped her chin upward. "Yes."

Cory bent and scooped her up in his arms. "Get the door, Jack. I'm about to bust."

Jack jerked the door open. "You and me both."

Cory took her to the center of the living room and laid her down on the rug in front of a monstrous stone fireplace.

The soft wool rug warmed Bunny's back, and she stretched her arms above her head, feeling sexier and more uninhibited by the minute. "I thought you were going to show me the bedroom."

Cory ripped his shirt open, popping buttons across the room. "Too far." He dragged the shirt off and flung it to the floor.

Bunny rose to her knees and unbuckled his

belt, slipping it through the loops. "In a hurry, cowboy?" she murmured as she flicked the top button loose on his jeans and slid his zipper down.

"Holy hell." Jack unbuttoned the first couple of buttons on his shirt, gave up and pulled it over his head, tossing it onto a nearby leather chair. "Cory, old buddy, I think we actually won the auction the other night."

"Agreed."

Bunny reached for Jack's belt and yanked it free. "You guys talk too much, and you're overdressed." She unzipped Jack's jeans and eased his cock free, running her tongue around the rim. "Need a written invitation?"

Cory and Jack leaped out of their boots and jeans and stood before her in all their naked, well-toned, muscular glory.

Bunny rose to her feet, her body quivering, every cell screaming for what the men had to offer. "You know, this isn't part of the auction deal. You don't have to go through with this."

"Do you think we'd be doing this with any other woman?" Cory asked.

"What if number forty-one had won the bid?" she teased.

"She wasn't going to." Jack grinned.

Bunny frowned. "How do you know?"

"We worked it all out with Audrey—" Jack's words were cut off when Cory jammed an elbow into his gut.

Bunny's hands shifted to fist on her hips. "What do you mean?"

Cory lifted one of her hands. "We wanted you to win."

Jack took her other hand. "No other woman would do."

"You don't even know me." Bunny shook her head. "If this is some cruel trick, I don't want any part of it."

"Look at this place." Cory motioned with his free hand to the interior of his log cabin. "Do you think I needed the extra money you pay me to deliver flowers?"

Bunny glanced around, knowing the answer before she shook her head. "You were playing me?"

"Not playing you. Getting to spend a little more time with you."

"What about you?" She turned an angry glare on Jack.

"I don't have a single girlfriend and my mother's allergic flowers. Do you think all those bud vases were for her? They're lined up in a closet in my bedroom. Every one of those roses reminded me of you."

Bunny's frown deepened. This was too much. Though she wanted to believe them, she couldn't. They'd set her up, playing her all along. For what? A quick fuck? Fooled by a man once, she wasn't falling for any more lies. "I want my bud vases back."

"At least give us a chance." Jack smiled, holding out his hand.

Butterflies fluttered in Bunny's gut and her hands

trembled. "You lied to me and tricked me into bidding on you and winning. For what? I don't need men in my life who lie. As far as I'm concerned, this date is over." Bunny glanced around the room, searching for her clothes, before she remembered they were still out on the porch. Cold feet chilled her to the core and her heart raced. "I divorced the last man who kept secrets from me. I don't need another man who can't tell me the truth."

"Bunny, darlin'. We only wanted to get you alone. We meant no harm." Cory slid his arms around her waist and pulled her back against his front. "Stay for the night. Let us prove how much we care."

Jack stepped in front of her and took her hand and cupped her breast with his other. "Please."

With Cory's cock nudging the crease between her butt cheeks, and Jack tweaking her nipple to a hard nub, Bunny fought a losing battle between her body and her mind. "I shouldn't trust you two."

"She wants us." Jack smiled and stepped closer until his shaft pressed into her belly.

"Don't rush her," Cory said, as his hands dipped lower to thread through the hairs covering her sex.

"I don't know..." Bunny leaned her head back against Cory's chest. "No more lies?"

"Honey, we won't lie to you ever again." Jack guided her hand to his chest and made and X with her finger. "Cross my heart."

"Cross my heart," Cory echoed.

"Well..." Bunny wavered. "The rug did feel pretty good."

Cory's fingers found her folds, parting them.

"And I'd hate to leave on a bad note." Bunny sucked a breath through her teeth when Cory strummed her clit with a long, supple digit.

"And we want to show you a good time, like you deserve." Jack blew his hot, moist breath against her nipple, then touched it with the tip of his tongue.

Every cell ignited inside her, pushing her past her misgivings. "What the hell." Bunny reached behind her and grasped Cory's cock in her hand. "Show me you know how to use this."

Cory chuckled. "Jack, I believe our sweet little rose is blooming."

"Glory be!" Jack picked her up and swung her around.

Bunny wrapped her arms around his neck and held on, deliciously aware of her naked breasts pressed against the coarse hairs on his chest.

"You're way too pretty a blossom to stay in the shade." He kissed her soundly and stood her on her feet.

"I don't know about pretty." Bunny laughed, breathless. "Ray didn't think…"

Cory pulled her into his arms. "Ray was a dumbass who didn't deserve you." He lifted her off her feet and laid her gently on the rug before he dropped down beside her. "Jack and I are going to show you how you should be loved."

Come to think of it, the fact Ray and his pretty young bride were getting married the following day didn't hurt much at all. Not with two very attractive men about to do wicked things to her body. Bunny smiled up at Cory, curling her arms around his neck. "I'd really like that." *Even if it's only for tonight.*

Jack lay down on her other side and trailed his hand along her arm and across her ribs to cup her breast. "I can't believe you're here with us."

Bunny choked on a laugh. "You? I can't believe I'm here with two of the most beautiful men in Texas. And naked."

"Believe it, darlin'." Cory bent to touch his lips to hers, his tongue gliding between her teeth to thrust against hers.

Leaning up on one hand, he parted her legs with the other, his fingers brushing her inner thigh, all the way up to her curly thatch.

Her pussy quivered and she let her knees fall open.

Jack pinched her nipple gently, making it pebble into a hard little knot. "You have beautiful breasts, Bunny. They're perfect." He cupped one, weighing it in his palm. "Grapefruit." Jack grinned and took the fruit into his mouth, pulling gently.

Bunny arched her back, pressing deeper into his mouth, her insides igniting into a raging lust.

Cory parted her folds and stroked a finger across her most sensitive bundle of nerves.

Bunny moaned, her body writhing beneath his touch.

"Like that?" Cory kissed her lightly then swept his lips down her neck line, leaving a trail of quivering skin and vibrating nerves in his wake.

By the time he reached her mons, Bunny could barely breathe.

Jack stole over her and pressed his mouth to hers. "Cory will have you screaming, but after that, it's my turn, and I'll leave you begging for more."

"What's that?" Cory's breath stirred the hairs over her. "A challenge?"

"Oh, please," Bunny whispered, reaching for Cory, her fingers lacing through his hair, urging him down.

"Begging already?" Cory's tongue tapped her clit, then swirled around it in a long, sensuous stroke.

"Yes!" Bunny's back arched off the floor. "There. That's it."

While Cory's mouth laid siege to her clit, two large fingers slid inside her slick channel.

She raised her knees, giving him better access.

Jack looped a hand around her thigh, tugging it back.

Cory sucked her clit into his mouth, laving it with his tongue.

Tension peaked, and Bunny shot over the edge, crying out in the cavernous living room, her voice echoing off the timbers.

Jack chuckled beside her, his fingers trailing down her torso. "Now, let me show you how it's done."

Bunny lay panting, her mind completely mush, her body shaking from the most unbelievable orgasm she'd ever experienced. "Oh, sweet Jesus. I didn't know it was supposed to feel this good, until you two came along."

Jack leaned up on his elbow and smiled down at

her, tucking a strand of her hair behind her ear. "Now you do. You deserve so much more."

"Yes, darlin'." Cory slapped her thigh and kissed her mound. "Anything less is robbing you."

She smiled and stretched, feeling decidedly decadent. "Is there more?"

Jack and Cory laughed out loud.

"Honey, there's a lot more where that came from."

Bunny leaned up on her elbows, her eyelids drifting down to half-mast. "I want to participate this time, not just be on the receiving end."

Cory grinned. "Glad to hear that, babe." He rose to his knees between her legs and his cock jutted straight out, thick, hard and pulsing. "'Cause I'm in a heap of hurt."

"And so am I." Jack got up on his knees as well.

"There are two of you and only one of me, and since you've had more experience at this, why don't you show me how it's done?" Her brows rose, anticipation and excitement bubbling up inside her.

Cory nodded. "That, we can do."

"Do you like playing a little rough?" Jack asked.

Bunny's eyes widened. The idea was new and strangely appealing. "I don't know. How rough?"

"We won't hurt you," Cory assured her.

She shrugged and grinned. "Okay then. Show me what you've got."

Cory glanced across at Jack.

If Bunny didn't know better, they had some unwritten, unspoken communication going on.

Jack reached for his jeans, yanked a condom out of his back pocket and tossed it to Cory.

While Cory shielded himself, Jack grabbed Bunny around the hips and flipped her over.

Bunny squealed and came up on her hands and knees. "A little warning next time," she groused, more titillated than bothered by the forceful handling.

Cory smacked her bare bottom, light enough not to hurt, but hard enough to send tingles throughout her body. "Shush, woman. You're our toy to be played with now."

"Is that so?"

Cory slapped her again. It sounded worse than it felt.

Bunny's pussy creamed in response. She'd never known she'd like being spanked. "Oooh. Spank me again."

Cory slapped her ass then positioned himself behind her, with his cock pressed against her pussy. "Are you ready?"

Bunny leaned back, trying to get him to enter. "More than. But what about Jack?"

"He's got plans for you." Cory hesitated with his penis barely pressed into her.

Jack moved to kneel in front of Bunny, his cock bouncing in her face. "You want to participate?"

She stared at the large, thick shaft, her mouth watering. Her tongue swept across her lips. Bunny knew what he wanted and was more than ready to give it to him. "Are we going on another Ferris wheel ride?" she teased.

"Yes, ma'am." He moved closer.

Bunny stuck out her tongue and lapped the tip of Jack's cock.

Cory knelt behind her, his hands resting on her ass, parting her cheeks, his thumbs massaging her, moving closer to her tight anus. When he reached it, he poked one thumb in.

Bunny gasped, her mouth opening.

Jack thrust between her lips at the same time Cory drove his cock into her ultra-slick channel.

Her moan eased out around Jack's shaft as sensations rippled across her body.

"Ride her, Cory," Jack urged, pumping in and out of Bunny's mouth. His hands dug into her hair, pulling hard enough to stretch her scalp.

The hint of pain made Bunny tingle even more, her pussy contracting around Cory's cock as he pulled out to the tip, then thrust into her again.

With men coming at her from both ends, Bunny rode a tidal wave of sensations until she shot to the edge, hovering at the precipice, unable to breathe or move.

Jack thrust into her mouth one last time and pulled free.

Cory drove in once more and held her hips in a tight grasp, his cock buried to the hilt. Then he moaned and his shaft pulsed inside her.

Bunny's arms gave way, and she lowered her face to the rug, her ass still high in the air as Cory came inside her.

When his grip loosened, he eased her the rest of the way to the floor and spooned her body against his.

Jack lay down in front of her, his hand resting on her breast.

Bunny caught his cock in her hand and stroked its hard length. "You didn't come."

"I can wait." He smiled, though his face was tight, his dark eyes intense.

"What if I don't want to wait?" she asked.

Cory pulled out of her and eased her onto her back. "Are you sure?"

A muscle flickered in Jack's jaw. "I don't want to hurt you."

She spread her thighs wide. "Please. I'm begging you. Take me now." With a wicked smile, she winked.

Jack grabbed a condom from his discarded jeans, tore it open with his teeth and rolled it over his engorged penis. Then he lay between her legs and guided his cock to her entrance. "You're amazing," he said and slid into her in one long, slow stroke.

Bunny wrapped her legs around his waist and dug her heels into his buttocks. "Deeper."

"Are you sure?" Jack frowned, his body tense as if he was holding back. "I'm pretty big."

Cory snorted. "Like I'm not?"

"Please." Bunny increased the pressure on his butt cheeks, wanting all of him inside her and his balls slapping against her ass. She raised a hand to Cory's cheek. "And yes, you're big too." She chuckled. "Are you two always this competitive?"

"More so." Jack pulled out and sank back into her.

As Jack filled her, Bunny drew in a deep breath. "And you've shared a woman before?"

"Yes, but we were all a little drunk," Cory explained. "We all agreed we weren't going to make it a habit."

"Why?" Bunny asked as Jack withdrew and she could breathe again.

"She wasn't the right girl for us."

"And we weren't the right men for her. She was a one-man kinda woman."

"Was she insane? One man, when she could have had you both? Stupid woman." Bunny's legs clamped around Jack, dragging him back into her. "Faster, please."

Cory tapped Jack's arm. "You heard the woman. She has needs."

Bunny wanted to ask if she was the right woman for them, but she didn't want to put them on the spot if their answer was no.

Again, she had to remind herself this was a one-time deal. They were under no obligation to date her ever again. Her eyes burned with a sudden need to cry.

"Is he hurting you?" Cory leaned over her, his brows drawn together in a fierce frown.

"No." She laughed, the sound more of a sob. She'd never felt this cared for or pampered in her life. She'd never known a man, or men, who took the time to make her feel that same euphoric feeling that only came with an incredible orgasm. These two men knew how to treat a woman, how to make her scream and beg for more. They cared enough to make fore-play an art.

A tear slid from the corner of her eye.

"Jack, stop. You're hurting her."

Jack started to withdraw.

"No!" Bunny locked her ankles around his waist. "Faster, damn it."

Jack complied, pounding into her like a jackhammer.

Bunny closed her eyes, loving the force of each thrust, the heat building in the juices lining her channel and the ultimate slam, leading to Jack's release.

He pulled free and collapsed on the rug beside her, his fingers finding her clit, stroking.

"You don't have to." She squirmed, pressing into his hand.

Jack shook his head. "I like watching your face tense and your body come alive when we get you there."

"Makes us hard all over again." Cory nudged her bottom with the proof of his desire.

"You two are insatiable." Bunny gasped as Jack's finger found the spot and took her the rest of the way there. The pleasure so intense it was almost painful. Bunny grabbed his hand and stopped him, reveling in her pulsing release.

At last she fell back against the rug and lay spent, drained, and for the first time in her life completely satisfied. "That was so much better than my vibrator."

Jack and Cory laughed and pressed up against her.

After a few minutes, Cory lifted her and carried her into the bedroom. The three of them touched and fondled until they'd regained strength and the party began again.

Somewhere around two in the morning, Bunny slipped out of the bed, tiptoed across the living room and out onto the front porch where she quickly dressed. Then she pulled her cell phone from her purse with the intention of calling Mona.

No service.

"Going somewhere?" A gravelly, deep voice rumbled from the doorway.

Bunny stifled a scream and spun toward the sound.

Cory, dressed only in a pair of jeans, leaned against the doorframe, looking rumpled, sleepy and sexy as hell.

Her pulse increased, heat building in her body. "Oh, it's you."

A slow smile slid across his lips. "Expecting someone else?"

"No." She stared down at the phone. "Can't get a call through anyway."

Cory held out his hand. "Come back to bed."

Bunny clutched her purse to her chest. "It's after midnight. Our date is officially over."

"It doesn't have to be."

She swayed toward him, wanting to go back to bed with him and Jack, but the thought of waking up with these two men was too much. She'd want it to last even longer and longer still. Best to end it now, before they did.

"I have a wedding to work in a few hours."

"Screw the wedding." He reached for her again.

Bunny backed away. "I can't. It's my business."

"We'll get you there on time."

Bunny shook her head. "I need to go." She stared across at him, her eyes stinging, on the verge of tears. "Please."

Cory remained leaning on the doorframe a few moments longer, his blue eyes dark in the shadows. Finally, he straightened and nodded. "Okay. Let me get my keys."

He was back in less than a minute, wearing his boots and a T-shirt and carrying his keys.

"Jack?" Bunny started to ask.

"Asleep."

"Good." She climbed into Cory's convertible and settled back against the leather seat, closing her eyes.

The ride sped by and in too short a time, Cory pulled in front of her shop and switched off the engine.

When he started to reach for the door handle, she laid a hand on his arm. "You don't have to walk me up."

"The hell I don't."

"Please." She leaned across the seat and kissed him. "I can make it on my own."

He captured her face in his hands and stared hard into her eyes. "I know you can make it on your own.

It's one of the things I love most about you. You're independence and self-reliance."

"Then let me go. I'll be okay."

He stared a little longer and finally let go. "What should I tell Jack?"

She smiled and slid toward her door. "Tell him he was great and thanks."

Bunny hurried out of the convertible and up the stairs to her apartment without looking back, afraid that if she did, she'd lose her nerve and beg Cory to take her back to his place. When she'd let herself in and closed the door behind her, she leaned her back on the panel and listened. Somewhere in the back of her mind, she'd hoped Cory would follow her and ask her to come back with him.

Face it, girl—the date was just a date.

Bunny slid down the door and settled on the floor, letting the tears that had been burning in her eyes all the way back to town slide down her cheeks.

In the few hours she'd spent with Cory and Jack, she'd learned more about making love than in the entire time she'd been married. And damn it, she didn't want it to end.

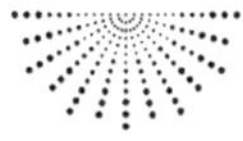

"That's the last of the arrangements," Charli said, carrying a small vase, which she set in the middle of the last empty table.

"Thanks, Charli," Bunny said from her perch at the top of the bridal arch. "I'll be done with this in just a minute, then we can leave."

"Not staying for the event?" Mona asked, her tongue pressing against the inside of her cheek.

"Hell, no." Bunny smiled. "After Ray blasted me at the garden party, I think he'd be appalled if I dared to invite myself."

"I'd love to see Ray's face if you sat in the front row." Mona giggled. "Jerk-face would have puppies."

"Shh, Mona. Jerk—Ray will be here any minute. I want to be out of here when he arrives. The wedding starts in less than two hours."

"Poor Chrissy has to spend the rest of her life

having sex with him." Mona's eyes narrowed. "Speaking of sex…"

"I'm not talking about last night. I told you all I'm going to tell you."

"That good, huh?" Charli piped in. "Back when Connor was playing dirty tricks on me, he had a couple of his buddies join the fun. I'll bet those two were in on it. Might not have seen their faces, but those chests…"

Bunny glared down at Charli.

Charli raised her hands. "What? You said there wasn't going to be any more dates with Cory and Jack."

"You could at least wait a few days before you start adding them to your list of sex partners in front of me."

"Yeah, Charli. Have a little respect for the lonely spinster." Mona grinned.

Bunny flung a rose bud at Mona. "You're not helping." She tucked the last spray of roses and baby's breath into the arch and climbed down from the stepladder. "There. Now we can leave."

Tired from her late night with the guys and wanting to see them again more than she could tell anyone, Bunny was ready to go back to her little, lonely apartment and wallow in a half gallon of rocky road ice cream. Alone.

They loaded her van with the stepladder and the supplies she'd used to create the fairytale wedding for Ray and Chrissy and went back into the chapel for one last glance.

Mona hooked her elbow and squeezed her arm. "They don't deserve what you did for them."

"I don't harbor ill feelings toward them. Maybe this is all working out for the best. Ray and I didn't click as a couple. It's just too bad we wasted so many years of our lives trying to make it work."

"It's too bad you spent so many years of your life getting him through dental school only for him to ditch you as soon as he finished." Charli tugged her arm. "Come on. I'm sure Kendall will be ready to close the shop and call it a day."

"She's an angel for volunteering to help out." Bunny smiled and turned toward the exit. "I'm glad I did Ray's wedding. It proves to me once and for all I was never in love with him in the first place. I think I was in love with the idea of being in love and being married."

"Now that you know what love is?" Mona waggled her brows. "Come on, you have to tell us something. We've been good all day."

"Really, Bunny. What are friends for but to share all the intimate details of each other's sex lives?" Charli waited for a few seconds, then rolled her eyes. "Forget it, Mona. She's not talking."

Bunny cast Charli a thankful look and patted Mona's arm. "I'm not ready. Maybe someday."

"They were that good." Mona sighed. "I knew it."

Oh yes, Jack and Cory had been so good it would be a long time before Bunny went on another date with any man. How could anyone measure up to what her two "dates" had done for her?

Hell, she'd have been better off not going out on that date. She'd been happily lonely, content to give her vibrator the occasional workout.

Now she couldn't even touch the cold, hard tool without thinking of how warm, thick and velvety smooth Jack and Cory had been in her hands and mouth, and…

Bunny climbed into the van with its bright pink swirling letters declaring it as the property of the Sweet Temptations Flower Shop.

"Another wedding." Mona slid into the middle seat and sighed. "I gotta quit helping you with these. It's too darned depressing. Always the florist, never the bride."

Charli chuckled, climbed into the passenger seat and slammed the door. "Always giving the flowers, never getting them? God, I'm glad Connor has a romantic streak in him."

A smile curved Bunny's lips. "You liked that arrangement of daisies he had me deliver to you at the Ugly Stick?"

Charli's eyes narrowed. "Your idea, or his?"

"All his." Bunny raised her hand. "I suggested carnations. He said you preferred daisies because they made you smile." Bunny's heart twisted at the man's sentiment. "You got a keeper in Connor."

Charli smiled. "I know. And he's not so stuffy he won't consider an occasional ménage."

Bunny cast a quick glance at Charli. "I didn't know he was kinky like that."

"Oh, he's quite the trickster. And there are more

threesomes and moresomes than you think in these parts."

"Right. Look at the Gray Wolf twins and Libby," Mona piped in.

"And the three O'Briens and Isabella." Charli laughed. "I bet she's kept really busy."

"Nothing wrong with multiples in a relationship," Mona said. "Wish I could find me one man, much less two."

Bunny shifted into drive and was just about to pull out of the church parking lot when Ray pulled up in a black Cadillac and blocked her way.

He climbed out, dressed in a crisp white shirt and his black tuxedo trousers. "Everything ready?" he asked.

Bunny climbed back out of her van and stood before Ray. "It is. Just as Chrissy wanted."

Ray sucked in a deep breath and let it out. "I'm just glad this will be over soon, and we won't have to deal with each other anymore."

"Does this mean you're going to shut me down after all?"

"Don't have to. I turned over my shares to the bank for a profit. They paid me ten grand for my half of the business."

Bunny's heart sank. "Without talking to me?"

"I'm a busy man. I don't have time to fool with you and your stupid shop. The bank took care of it. Now you'll have to answer to them. Seems to me they were looking at that location for possible expansion." Ray smirked.

Bunny bit down on her lip to keep from calling Ray a name.

"Bastard," Mona said behind her. "You never deserved Bunny, you rotten excuse of a coward."

Ray snorted. "I'm disappointed in what you've become."

"Careful, dentist." Charli joined them, her fists clenching. "Or I'll give you a little of what Bunny gave you the other night."

Ray pressed a hand to the bruise on his chin, glared at Charli, then faced Bunny again. "Your behavior the last couple days proves only one thing: you've become a first class slut."

"I warned him." Charli slugged Ray in the nose.

Ray squealed and clutched his broken nose, blood spurting out onto his white shirt. "Bitch!"

"Better clean that up before Chrissy gets here." Charli stood in front of him, her legs spread wide, daring him to do anything. "And never, ever fuck with my friends again."

Her lips twitching, Bunny grasped Charli's arm and tugged her toward the van. "Come on, he's not worth it."

Charli resisted for a second, then shrugged. "You're right. He's got little-dick syndrome."

The three women climbed into the van and left. A few minutes later, Bunny pulled up to the flower shop and parked in the alley beside it. "Thanks again, ladies. I couldn't have done it without you. And I mean it." She got out and hugged them both. "I don't suppose you two would like to go out to dinner as a celebration?" Anything to keep from being alone. Especially tonight.

Charli slung her purse over her shoulder. "I got a man waiting for me at home. And who knows what we'll do tonight. All your teasing about Cory and Jack has me horny as hell. Gotta go scratch that itch." She took off toward her truck without looking back.

"What about you, Mona?"

Mona heaved a sigh. "Sorry, I promised Molly O'Brien I'd do her hair this afternoon."

"After helping me all day?"

Mona shrugged. "I know, I should have put her off, but she sounded desperate."

Bunny nodded. "I understand."

"Maybe Kendall will be free tonight," Mona suggested.

"Right." Bunny doubted Kendall would be free when she had Ed to go home to. "You go on. I can unload myself."

"You're sure?" Mona asked.

"I'm sure." She'd rather be alone to think about what had happened last night. Reliving every moment had been difficult throughout the day.

Bunny carried the stepladder through the back door into her work area and hung it on hooks on the wall. "Hey, Kendall, I'm back," she called out.

As she walked through the back room lined with glass-fronted refrigerators, she took an automatic mental inventory of the flowers she stored there, noting the absence of roses. As she entered the front of the shop, Kendall was slinging her purse over her shoulder.

"Oh, Bunny. I'm so glad you're here."

"How was it today?"

"Great." Kendall handed her an envelope. "This was delivered to you. I have a date with Ed and can't stay, but I sold every last one of your pink, white and red roses. Gotta go. Bye." Kendall left through the front door, a big smile on her face.

"Probably gonna get some tonight," Bunny muttered, picturing her own small, empty bed upstairs. Then what Kendall had said about selling all her roses struck Bunny, and she ducked back into the workroom and let it sink in. "Holy smokes, she sure did." She'd have to order fresh stock on Monday as soon as the market opened. Her work never ended. But it was her livelihood and it helped keep a roof over her head.

Bunny wondered who the lucky girl was who'd gotten all those roses. With a sigh, she slid her finger in the back of the envelope and popped the flap open.

Inside was a beautiful note card with a picture of roses on the front.

Bunny's heart bumped unsteadily and settled into a fast pace. She flipped the note card open and read,

That which we call a rose

By any other name would smell so sweet

Come fair Bunny,

Be thou the rose that brightens our garden?

The flowing handwriting switched to strong, bold strokes. Bunny's heart lightened as she read,

I told Cory this was dumb, but whatever it takes to
Woo the fair Bunny, I'll go for.
Comest upstairs, fair rose by another name.
See? Sounds stupid, doesn't it?
Just remember, it's what's in our hearts that matters.

Her pulse pounding, Bunny glanced up at the sound of footsteps in her apartment above the shop.

Could it be? Would they really want to see her again? No strings, no auctions, no obligations?

Her hands shook, the note card rattling against her fingers.

A voice inside her head, shouted, *Go! Go! Go!*

Bunny spun and raced out the back door and up the steps to the tiny suite of rooms above the shop. When she reached the top of the stairs, her hand paused on the doorknob as she fought to catch her breath.

Then she flung the door wide, the rich, sweet smell of roses filling her senses.

Vases of roses lined every surface, and rose petals in every shade of red, white and pink carpeted her floor through the tiny living room into the bedroom.

A heavy thud was followed by a muttered curse.

Bunny grinned and slipped off her shoes, letting the velvet petals caress her toes as she closed the distance between the front door and the bedroom.

Candles lined her dresser, threatening to set fire to the vases of roses crammed between them. But it wasn't the candles that made her heart race. It was the two men wearing black tuxedos with no shirts beneath the jackets, lying across her bed, each with a single red rose clamped between his teeth.

Jack spit out his rose. "I said we should be naked." He jerked his head toward the other handsome man in the bed. "Cory said tuxes."

Cory grinned and twirled the rose stem between his fingers. "We compromised."

Jack flung out his arm. "Welcome home."

Her heart nearly bursting from her chest, Bunny whispered, "What are you doing here?"

Cory blinked. "Isn't it obvious?"

She shook her head. "I only paid for one date."

Jack climbed off the bed and gripped her hand, dragging her over to the end of the bed. "We don't want it to end at one date."

"But you don't have to. You're not obligated…"

Cory leaped to his feet and pulled her into his arms. "I told you, we *wanted* you to win us. It was just the beginning of our quest to win your heart."

Bunny glanced at Jack.

He nodded. "What he said. He's much better with words." Jack brushed the hair out of her face, tucking it behind her ear. "I only know what's in my heart. You're the gal for me."

"And me," Cory added. "You're the woman we want in our lives."

"So, what do you say?" Jack grinned.

"It's so sudden." Bunny pressed a hand to her pounding chest. This couldn't be happening. She pinched her arm and flinched. No. She wasn't asleep.

With a glance from Jack to Cory, she asked, "Both of you? You won't be jealous?"

"We both care about you," Cory said.

"And we're good enough friends we wouldn't do anything to bust that up," Jack continued.

"And we know what we want." Cory lifted her hand to his lips.

"You," Jack concluded.

"Say you'll give us a chance." Cory pressed her palm to his cheek.

"We got you roses," Jack said.

"Yes, you did." Bunny bit her lower lip, but she couldn't keep the smile from spreading across her face. "What if I lose the shop and have to move to find work?"

Cory shook his head. "Not happenin'."

She frowned. "How can you be sure?"

"We invested in it."

"You what?"

Jack jumped in, "We're partners, you, me and Cory."

Cory grinned. "We're going into the flower business."

Bunny's eyes widened. "You bought the note from the bank?"

"Yes, but we have it in writing that Bunny Leigh is to be the CEO and have all the decision-making authority on how the shop is run."

"We'll be silent investors," Jack said.

Bunny's heart lightened and she shook her head. "I can't imagine either one of you being silent."

"So are you good with it?"

"I'd like to have known before Ray told me he'd turned it over to the bank."

"We wanted to surprise you."

"Maybe use it as a carrot to win you over to our side."

Bunny laughed. "How can I resist?"

"Then you'll give us a chance?"

Her eyes filled with tears and she nodded. "Okay. We'll give this crazy, mixed up ménage a shot." When they lunged toward her, she held up a hand. "And if it doesn't work?"

"It will." Jack grabbed her hand and pulled her closer.

"We know what makes you happy." Cory slipped her purse off her shoulder and tossed it on a chair. He shoved his jacket off his shoulders. "A little stripping."

Jack shucked his jacket and pressed her hand to his chest. "A lot of skin."

Cory backed her to the end of the bed until her knees bumped the mattress. He grabbed the hem of her shirt and lifted it over her head. Then he clasped her in his arms and kissed her soundly. "And a whole lot of lovin'."

Bunny laughed and fell into their arms. "I believe I'm the luckiest woman in the world."

"Oh, you're gonna get lucky all right." Jack waggled his brows and ripped the pants right off his legs.

Cory did the same. "One of the perks of being a

stripper…quick-release clothes. Now, let us show you how much you're gonna love us."

If you enjoyed this book, try the other books in the Ugly Stick Saloon Series

Boots & Chaps (#1)

Boots & Sex Ed (#2)

Boots & Leather (#3)

Boots & Promises (#4)

Boots & Bareback (#5)

Boots & Dirty Tricks (#6)

Boots & Lace (#7)

Boots & Roses (#8)

Boots & Buckles (#9)

Boots & the Wishes (#10)

Boots & Twisters (#11)

Boots & the Bachelor (#12)

Boots & the Rogue (#13)

Boots & the Heartbreaker (#14)

Boots & Wings (#15)

BOOTS & BUCKLES

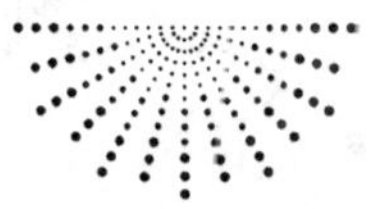

UGLY STICK SALOON SERIES BOOK #9

by Elle James
New York Times Bestselling Author

writing as

Myla Jackson

BOOTS & BUCKLES
UGLY STICK SALOON
New York Times Bestselling Author
ELLE JAMES
writing as
MYLA JACKSON

CHAPTER ONE

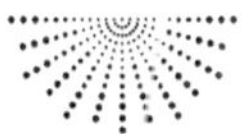

Grant saw her as soon as he stepped through the door. Just like it had been when he'd seen her for the first time, he'd been drawn to Mona's smile and the way she moved with a sexy flare she wasn't even aware of.

The three years since he'd last been to Temptation hadn't changed her much. Perhaps she was a little thinner, but she was just as beautiful as the day they'd met at the Ugly Stick Saloon during Tri-County Rodeo week. He and his then-partner, Dalton Faulkner, had been there for the rodeo. She'd been helping out at the Ugly Stick, waiting tables and serving drinks to rowdy cowboys fresh off the adrenaline rush of roping steers, riding bulls or broncs.

He chose the table in the back of the saloon because it *wasn't* one that Mona was servicing. His waitress, Kendall, was a sweet young thing he didn't recognize from his last visit to the saloon. She wore a diamond engagement ring on her finger and didn't take any lip or advances from the horny men raising hell after a tough day in the saddle.

"This place is great." His new team roping partner, Sam Whitefeather, tipped his long neck and swallowed the last of the beer in one gulp, slapped the bottle on the table and pushed to his feet. "You stickin' around for a while?"

"Yeah, why?"

"Could you order me another? I'm gonna hit the latrine." Sam reached for his wallet.

Grant held up his hand. "I'll get this round. Go."

He'd skipped the last two years' rodeos here because he couldn't bring himself to face Mona. The first year, because his life had been a mess, his career as a team roper at an end when he and Dalton had parted ways, and his bronc riding on the verge of collapse.

If not for Sam, he'd have found some bottle to crawl into and given up on everything. It took him the next couple years of total focus and concentration to regain his credibility and top rating in the competitions. Only then had he felt like he could return and see if there was anything left to salvage between him and Mona.

The woman foremost on his mind walked by carrying a tray of beer mugs and long necks, and his heart flipped over, reminding Grant of everything he'd lost and all the mistakes he'd made. He tipped his hat lower over his forehead, not ready to let her see him. Not sure what he expected to get out of coming back to Temptation. Would she ever forgive him for making promises he didn't keep?

Mona plunked her tray of empty beer bottles and mugs on the bar and gave Libby, the bartender, her order for the next round to be delivered.

Audrey Anderson, the owner of the Ugly Stick Saloon, slipped in beside her, carrying her own tray of empties. "Mona, thanks so much for helping out during rodeo week."

"No, Audrey. I should be thanking you. I don't know what I would have done without you."

"You really don't think Old Man Spillman will extend the lease on your salon?"

"I've already asked. I have a thirty-day option to buy and Spillman is ready to sell. If I don't agree to buy it in that thirty days, the old coot is going to take the first reasonable offer."

"How much are you short?"

"I have to come up with at least another grand to add to my meager savings before the bank will even consider loaning me the money to buy the building."

"I can spot you the money."

Mona shook her head. "I can't let you do that. You've already done so much for me and half the people in town. If I can't find a way to earn the money, I don't deserve to buy the salon."

"I could use you all week, if that will help."

"I'm all yours. I can come in after six every evening when I close the Shear Safari."

"Make it at least by nine and stay until midnight. That's when things are craziest and the men tip better." Audrey emptied her tray and slid behind the counter to help Libby fill her next round of orders.

Libby loaded Mona's tray and nodded. "You're good to go."

Mona lifted the heavy tray, balancing it carefully.

"Oh, and Mona," Audrey called out, "if you're interested in making more in a single night, I might have some exotic dancing gigs coming up. The rodeo winners usually hire some of the girls to dance at their parties."

Mona bit her lip. She'd danced for Audrey before, but now that she had her own business as a hair stylist, she'd decided the dancing jobs might offend potential customers. But with her salon at risk of closing, a girl had to take risks she normally wouldn't. "Let me know, and I'll think about it."

Audrey nodded. "I will. And no worries if you decide not to do it."

"Thanks." Mona turned and wove her way through the rowdy cowboys, some still wearing jeans and boots covered in rodeo dust. Others had taken the extra time to come showered, polished and dressed in their pearl-buttoned snap shirts, sporting their trophy belt buckles won that day or on the circuit.

Mona had her ass pinched more times than she could count. After a three-year sabbatical on dating, she'd about convinced herself she should try it again. Or rather Bunny Leigh's experience with the date she'd bid on at the Annual Cowboy Auction had convinced Mona it was time to get over the cowboy she'd foolishly given her heart to, and move on.

But now wasn't good. Not during the circus of Tri-County Rodeo week. She'd learned her lesson three years ago not to believe a rodeo cowboy any farther than she could throw him. She'd made the mistake of falling in love with a very handsome team roper. Like all the cry-in-your-beer songs played, he'd broken her heart.

Mona served the cowboys with a polite smile, enough to get a good tip, but not enough to encourage them to ask her out. She picked up the empty bottles from a table, setting them onto her empty tray.

"Have you seen the news?" one of the cowboys said to the other.

With the band playing loud enough to make the men shout to be heard, Mona couldn't help over-hearing their conversation.

"Nah, haven't been near a television for two days. What's up?"

"Raleigh's competin' on broncs, and he and the Indian are paired up for team ropin'."

"Whatever happened between him and his team ropin' partner Faulkner? Not that I'm sorry they busted up. Gives the rest of us a fighting chance to win."

"Faulkner is riding bulls these days. He's here too. Should be up on the bulls tomorrow."

Mona's hand shook. The bottle she'd just grabbed slipped from her fingers and bounced off the table.

The cowboy sitting in the seat beside her grabbed the bottle before it hit the floor and grinned up at her. "Careful there, pretty thing." He set the bottle on her tray and winked. "Don't suppose you'd dance with this old cowboy, wouldja?"

Her heart pounding against her ribs and her knees wobbling, Mona could only shake her head before she turned and hurried away.

She didn't know how she'd gotten back to the bar with all the bottles and mugs intact. Tossing the empties in the trash, she slid her tray across the bar and leaned against the counter, afraid her knees would buckle and she'd fall flat on her face.

"Hey, sweetie, you look as if you've seen a ghost." Bunny Leigh sat in the barstool beside her and frowned. "What's wrong?"

"Oh, Bunny, I just heard *they're* gonna be here."

"Who?" Bunny glanced around the saloon. "Where?"

Mona turned her back to the bar and stared around the shadowy interior of the saloon, searching and thankfully not finding them. "Grant Raleigh and Dalton Faulkner. They're competing in the rodeo!"

"Grant and Dalton?" Bunny's brows rose. "As in the love-'em-and-cheat-'em cowboys who broke your heart three years ago?"

Letting out a long slow breath, Mona fought to steady her racing pulse. "They're the ones." Well, at least one of them broke her heart. Grant.

Bunny spun on her stool and studied the crowd of cowboys, a fierce glare pressing her brows together.

"Where are they? I want to give them a piece of my mind."

She looked so much like a bull terrier guarding her bone that Mona laughed. "I doubt they'll show up around here. They're big shots now. Grant's won just about every bronc riding competition on the circuit and all the western wear outfitters are clamoring for him to represent them. And Dalton's been the reigning bull rider with his own line of boots. I doubt he'll have time to stop by for a beer."

"That and Grant's wife probably has some pull in keeping him home at night." Bunny snorted. "Would have been nice if he'd let you know he was engaged before he and Dalton started dating you."

"I should have known better than to date rodeo cowboys." Mona's lips twisted. "My mamma warned me about them a long time ago. Guess I had to learn for myself."

Audrey returned to the bar, followed by Charli Sutton. Both women set their empty trays behind the bar.

"The band is on break. It's that time, ladies," Audrey called out.

Libby and Audrey cleared the bar quickly and turned on the music for the night's performance. Audrey, Charli, Lacey, Kendall and Libby climbed up on the bar.

Audrey waved to Mona. "Come on, you know the routine."

Mona shook her head.

Bunny shoved her forward. "Get up there and

show them that you don't care about them anymore. You've moved on. There are dozens of cowboys in this room that would give their left nut to be with you."

"Yeah, and then they'll move on to the next rodeo, the next buckle bunny—no offense."

"None taken." Bunny grinned. "Get up there and have some fun."

Mona hesitated a second longer, glancing around the saloon, half-hoping she would see Dalton and Grant at the same time as she prayed they'd stay clear of the Ugly Stick throughout the rodeo.

As the music started, Mona threw her doubts to the Texas wind, hopped up on the bar and danced to the strains of "Save a Horse, Ride a Cowboy".

To hell with falling for heartbreakers. Tonight she'd break a few of her own.

SAM STEPPED out of the latrine to the sound of raucous shouting and loud bump-and-grind music. All the cowboys were turned toward the bar where the waitresses danced in unison in short-shorts, tight tank tops, cowboy hats and cowboy boots.

"Nice." Sam stood back several deep in the crowd, grinning. He'd never been to this part of Texas and the Ugly Stick Saloon had proven to be one of the friendliest bars he'd ever been inside. Not all bars welcomed Native Americans, though he preferred to be referred to as a Lakotan, but he'd felt right at home among the cowboys here.

And the pretty brunette waitress on the end seemed to smile right at him. What would it take to get that one to dance with him?

The woman in the middle wearing bright red, metal-studded cowboy boots, called out, "Catch a hat and dance with one of the lovely ladies of the Ugly Stick." The song ended, the ladies all yelled, "Yee-haw!" and flung their hats into the crowd.

Standing six feet five inches, Sam had no trouble snatching the one thrown by the brunette on the end and considered it a sign from *Wakatanka*, the Great Spirit, that he was meant to meet this woman and dance with her.

The cowboys parted to allow him to pluck the waitress off the bar and set her on her feet.

"Hello, I'm Mona Daley." She stuck out her hand.

"Sam Whitefeather." He plunked her hat on her head, took her hand and shook it. Someone bumped her from behind and she fell against his chest. Sam chuckled and held her steady until she got her feet under her and straightened her hat. He liked the way she smelled of honeysuckle and citrus.

The band struck up a slow song and the cowboys who'd caught the hats led the waitresses onto the dance floor. Sam followed, Mona's hand held snuggly in his.

She glanced up at him with pretty brown eyes. "Do you two-step?"

In answer, he lifted her hand, rested his other hand on the small of her back and swept her onto the dance floor, thanking his sister for insisting he help her learn how to dance. With their father working two jobs to make ends meet and feed them as well as the horses, Sam filled the gap his mother's early demise had created. Now that Gemma was out of high school and halfway through college at University of North Dakota, Sam could have a little fun and loosen up on his sense of responsibility for his kid sister.

Ah hell, who was he trying to kid? Gemma was part of the reason he'd gotten into rodeoing. It helped pay her way through school and kept his father out of debt. And none of it would have been possible if Grant hadn't collapsed in a drunken stupor outside a bar in Minot, North Dakota, during rodeo week.

He owed his current way of life to Grant, but the feeling was mutual. If Sam hadn't picked him up out of the gravel, shoved him into his truck and taken him to the Whitefeather Ranch, Grant might have died of exposure that night in the parking lot. And if not exposure, he might have crawled back into the bottle he'd been wallowing in and lost everything.

Now, Sam and Grant were on top of the rodeo world, winning big cash prizes and sponsorship deals at every rodeo. Grant pushed them as if he had an evil spirit on his tail he couldn't shake.

Sam suspected it had something to do with his ex-wife and his ex-partner. Only Grant had never filled him in on those parts of his past and Sam hadn't pushed.

With the pretty Mona in his arms, he didn't want

to look back, only forward to this dance and maybe more.

"Are you with the rodeo?" Mona asked with a smile.

"I am."

Her smile faded a bit then reappeared. "That's nice. What events do you participate in?"

"Team roping and bull ridin'." He inhaled her scent again, liking the way it wafted around him as they moved in a wide circle around the dance floor.

"You must meet a lot of people on the circuit," she commented, her gaze leaving his, her smile appearing more strained.

"I do. But none as pretty as you." His hand tightened around hers.

"Uh-huh. I'll bet you say that to all the girls you dance with." This time her smile was gone and she gazed directly into his eyes.

"No, just the ones who deserve it." He spun her away from him and back into his arms, holding her closer, his hips moving against hers. "Do you have a problem with rodeo cowboys?"

"Not anymore." She tossed her hair back over her shoulder. "You know, once burned, don't stand so close to the fire."

"And a rodeo cowboy burned you?" His fingers squeezed hers.

"Something like that." Her gaze went past him, as if looking into her memories.

He leaned close and whispered into her ear, "I'm

not here to burn you, Mona. I only want to dance with you."

She blinked up at him, her eyes shimmering with unshed tears. "Then shut up and dance."

Sam's chest tightened at the sadness he witnessed in her valiant attempt to pretend to be happy and carefree. This woman who fit so well against his body had been hurt badly by someone. The protector in him wanted to find that someone and break every bone in his body.

As the music came to a halt, Sam didn't want to let go. "One more dance?"

She shook her head. "Sorry, I have to get back to the tables. Those men can get pretty thirsty."

He held on to her hand as she spun away, dragging her back to his side. "Where can I find you during the day? I'd like to see you again."

"Sorry, I don't go out with rodeo cowboys." When she tried to jerk her hand free, he pulled her against his chest and kissed her lips.

GRANT'S HEART squeezed in his chest as Mona danced on the bar with the other women of the Ugly Stick Saloon and when she'd tossed her hat, he wanted to be the one to catch it, but he held back. The timing wasn't right. He wanted to get her alone and talk to her in private. See how she was, if she still had any feelings for him. If not, he knew he had to move on. This wouldn't be the place where he'd set down roots and retire. Not if he couldn't have Mona at his side.

When his partner had caught her hat and escorted her to the dance floor, Grant's gut knotted. Sam was as close as a friend could be. He's saved his sorry ass from self-destruction. And now he was dancing with the only woman Grant had ever loved.

When the music came to a halt, Grant rose to his feet, with some half-baked thought of going to Mona and demanding she not fall in love with his partner on the tip of his tongue.

Then Sam bent and kissed Mona. On her lips.

The air sucked out of Grant's lungs in a whoosh and he collapsed back in his chair.

Mona's eyes rounded and she reached up and slapped Sam in the face so hard the clap could be heard over the rumble of music and conversation of the rodeo cowboys. All eyes turned toward the pair on the dance floor. Sam's jaw tightened momentarily, then he smiled and dipped his head. "My apologies, ma'am."

The room erupted into loud raucous laughter and cowboys slapped Sam's back on his way back to the table he shared with Grant.

As Sam took his seat, he rubbed his cheek. "I deserved that."

Grant grunted, afraid if he said anything, he'd reveal more than he wanted. Hopefully, the slap on the face would discourage his partner from wanting to see Mona again.

As Sam rubbed the bright red handprint on his cheek, his face split in a grin. "That lady's got spunk. I'm gonna ask her out."

ABOUT THE AUTHOR

Twenty years of livin' and lovin' on a South Texas ranch raising horses, cattle, goats, ostriches and emus left an indelible impression on Myla Jackson, one she likes to instill in her red-hot stories. Myla pens wildly sexy, fun adventures of all genres including historical westerns, medieval tales, romantic suspense, contemporary romance and paranormal beasties of all shapes and sexy sizes. She lives in the tree-covered hills of Northwest Arkansas with her husband of more than 20 years and her muses—the human-wanna-be canines—Chewy and Sweetpea.

To learn more about Myla Jackson and her alter ego Elle James visit:

www.mylajackson.com
mylajackson@mylajackson.com

Tomb Raider Trouble

Trouble with Harry

Trouble with Will

Trouble with Mitch

Bound and Tied

Honor Bound

Duty Bound

River Bound

Paranormal

Shewolf

Thorn's Kiss

Sex, Lies & Vampire Hunters

Ugly Stick Saloon Series

Boots & Chaps (#1)

Boots & Sex Ed (#2)

Boots & Leather (#3)

Boots & Promises (#4)

Boots & Bareback (#5)

Boots & Dirty Tricks (#6)

Boots & Lace (#7)

www.ingramcontent.com/pod-product-compliance
Lightning Source LLC
Chambersburg PA
CBHW070958120726
47910CB00004B/1285